TSERING YANGKYI was born in Shigatse, Tibet, in 1962. She graduated from the Tibetan Language and Literature department of Tibet University in 1987, since which time she has worked as a middle school teacher in Lhasa. Tsering Yangkyi is one of the most recognized names in the Tibetan literary world. She began publishing fiction in the 1980s and has built up a body of work that concerns itself first and foremost with women and the underclass of Tibetan society. She began *Flowers of Lhasa*, her first novel, in 2009, and it tooks seven years to complete. When it was published in 2016, it became only the second novel by a Tibetan woman. In Tibet, the publication of her novel was immediately met with widespread acclaim, from critics and readers alike.

CHRISTOPHER PEACOCK holds a PhD from Columbia University. He is a translator and a scholar of modern Chinese and Tibetan literatures. His translations of modern Tibetan fiction have appeared in journals including *Chinese Literature Today*, *Ploughshares Solos*, *Pathlight*, and *Two Lines*. He is the translator of Tsering Döndrup's *The Handsome Monk and Other Stories*, one of the first collections of Tibetan fiction available in English.

TSERING YANGKYI

FLOWERS OF LHASA

A Novel

Translated from the Tibetan by

Christopher Peacock

BALESTIER PRESS
LONDON · SINGAPORE

Balestier Press
Centurion House, London TW18 4AX
www.balestier.com

Flowers of Lhasa
Original title: མེ་ཏོག་དང་རྩི་ལམ།
Copyright © Tsering Yangkyi, 2013
English translation copyright © Christopher Peacock, 2022

First published by Balestier Press in 2022

This book has been selected to receive financial assistance from English-PEN's PEN Translates programme, supported by Arts Council England.
English PEN exists to promote literature and our understanding of it,
to uphold writers' freedoms around the world, to campaign against
the persecution and imprisonment of writers for stating their views, and
to promote the friendly co-operation of writers and the free exchange of ideas.
www.englishpen.org

A CIP catalogue record for this book is available from the British Library.

ISBN 978 1 913891 22 0

Cover design by Sarah and Schooling

This book is a work of fiction. The literary perceptions and
insights are based on experience, all names, characters, places,
and incidents either are products of the author's imagination
or are used fictitiously.

FLOWERS OF LHASA

One

1

As the route circling the Jokhang Temple, the Barkhor is the heart of the old city of Lhasa, and the countless lively alleyways that weave in and out of the main thoroughfare are always teeming with people. Shasarzur was one such lively alley, but the restaurant tucked away in a corner of it—"Butri's Tibetan Cuisine"—had been struggling for business of late. Butri, the owner, had opened up early, but she'd barely had a customer come through the door. She cast envious glances in the direction of the Chinese restaurant over the street, which was packed from the minute it opened in the morning. Thinking about her own floundering business, she heaved a dejected sigh. She heated up the leftover sweet tea from the day before but lost her appetite for it after only a sip. Setting the cup down, she pondered the plight of her restaurant, racking her brains trying to come up with a way to get business going. This was not a problem that she had just thought of; it had been weighing on her day and night ever since her customer base had started to decline. The morning trade had been virtually non-existent recently and it was only in the afternoon that a handful of regulars started to drift in. These regulars consisted of old men who had retired from near-defunct businesses and neighbourhood idlers with barely two pennies to rub together. Since they wouldn't brave the classier establishments,

Butri's little restaurant was the best place for them to play their dice and their mahjong.

That day saw the first snowfall of the year in Lhasa, City of the Gods. People awoke to discover the city's alleyways completely blanketed in snow, which kept coming down for the whole day. Of course, there's nothing surprising about it snowing in the Land of Snows, but this first snowfall brought some moisture to the dry city air, and people hoped it might provide some relief from the flu season. The alley was normally abuzz with people—men, women, young and old—but that day it belonged entirely to the children, who were all busy getting in snowball fights and building their snowmen, filling the street with ringing laughter. Some mischievous kid hurled a snowball at the glass door of Butri's restaurant, making her jump out of her seat. She ran outside to chase them off, yelling furiously. "Little hooligans! You should all be in school!" The children scattered with a burst of cheeky laughter, glancing back at her over their shoulders. As she watched them run off, Butri thought to herself, *It's true what they say—you always get kicked when you're down. Business is slow, and now even the kids are pushing me around!* Her anger increased. The children were out of sight by that point, but she still picked up a lump of coal from the doorway and hurled it after them, just to soothe her temper. The pitch-black coal looked so out of place atop the freshly fallen snow in the alley, pristine and pearly. It made her think how easy it is to turn white to black, and how impossible it is to do the reverse. The change in weather didn't change the old men's gaming habits in the slightest: in the afternoon, Grandpa Tenpa shuffled through the door of the restaurant, rubbing his hands together.

"Butri, aren't the boys here yet?"

Butri glanced at the clock on the wall.

"It's just gone one o'clock, Grandpa Tenpa, they're probably still having lunch. You're a bit early today, aren't you?" Her expression was unwelcoming and irked. Grandpa Tenpa, not noticing Butri's demeanour—or perhaps just ignoring it—sat himself down without any hesitation and took a pack of Flying Horse cigarettes from his pocket. He lit one up and began puffing thick clouds of bluish smoke, then put his hand to the cold stove.

"It's freezing out, Butri, and it's snowing! It'd be lovely to warm myself by a nice fire on a day like this, and you haven't even got the stove going yet. Get it lit, would you, and can you get me a bowl of noodles? All the teahouses around the Barkhor are packed today, 'cause of the snow. I haven't even had lunch yet."

The old man's arrival wasn't well-timed. She still hadn't got over her anger at those kids in the street throwing snowballs at her door. She snorted irritably.

"Tenpa-la, as you ought to know, business is bad, and the price of the bloody coal has gone up. It's hard to get by when I've got no money coming in. You lot sit in here all day and don't order anything except a few Lhasa Beers. To tell you the truth, the money I get from that is barely enough to cover the cost of my fuel." She continued to grumble as she went to prepare the fire.

When Butri had first opened the restaurant, she was in the prime of her youth: fresh-faced, slim, and beautiful. She could sing, she could dance, she drank toasts with her customers, and she could hold her own when it came to the drinking, too. In those days, the alley was packed with Tibetan restaurants, teahouses, and bars, each little place with a sign above reading XX Teahouse or XX Restaurant. Apart from a handful of big and famous places, the XX Restaurants and XX Teahouses were, in reality, just places to get a cup of sweet tea and some noodles in the morning. Most of their few customers were like cats waiting for mice, biding their time until the afternoon when they could go and play their dice and drink their beer—or play their mahjong and drink their beer. There were a lot of joints like these, but none of them could compare with Butri's place. Her restaurant was overflowing with drinkers, and her purse was overflowing with hundreds.

Before long, all the drinking had taken its toll on her slender and graceful figure, and she had become a true tavern landlady. Then, when the customers came, they would mutter amongst themselves: "It's that ugly old mug again. She looks worse every time I see her. If we can't see any new faces around here, might as well go somewhere else to drink. She doesn't know any of the popular songs, and she's no good at the old arias, either. Always the same stuff—if it's not 'Let's Get Together' then it's 'Kelzang-la.' I'm sick of those bloody songs. Butri's lost her looks and there's no end to Kelzang-la." The flow of those fickle customers soon dried up. She racked her brains for solutions and tried hiring waitresses from the pool of young women who came from the country to the city to make money. But they were just as fickle as the customers: "We'd make more waitressing at a Chinese restaurant than here. In fact we'd make plenty unloading goods down at Lhalu Bridge, and without much more effort!" Never mind a full-time employee, a waitress who would see out the month was a rarity. Butri thought of everything she could. She prettied herself up, sporting a necklace of coral beads and adorning her fingers with fake gold rings. She wore a new outfit every day, she perfumed her body—and the inside of the restaurant, too. She clung to the hope that the customers would come back, but her business was like a waning moon.

Since she could barely support herself, she shut up shop and went back to her hometown, hoping to dig up some help for the restaurant. But most of the young people from the village had gone to the city to find jobs, leaving the elderly and the children with all the farm work—so where was Butri going to find this potential waitress? She went from door to door with a handbag full of sweets, giving out a handful to all the old folks and kids and asking them if they knew of any young women who would want to come work in the city. When she went back home to see her mother, she said to Butri, "The countryside isn't like it used to be, dear. Workers are hard to find these days. People used to worry about not finding their daughter a husband, but nowadays most young people from the village won't work in the fields after they graduate middle school, they disappear off to the city. Young women are very rare now and the men can't find wives. The women that stick around aren't the prettiest and they're not the best workers, but they've still got men queuing up to take them. So how on earth are you going to find a waitress here? No matter how dreary it is, this place is your home, where your land is. What's so great about the city? Why don't you come back? As long as we've got the land, you needn't worry about starving." Tears welled up in her eyes, but Butri gave her no reply. Without so much as a glance over shoulder, she set off back to the city.

Only after old Tenpa's dice partners had all showed up did Butri get the stove going. The dice players commenced their game. Dice is a rowdy affair: they whooped and hollered and quarrelled as they slammed their cups down on the table, calling out all those prescribed sayings that are part and parcel of any round of dice. But no matter how rowdy they got, the old men came early and left early, and only drank ten or so Lhasa Beers between them. Nevertheless, they were still regulars, and their money just about kept her afloat, so she made sure to keep the stingy old codgers happy.

It was the weekend, and it was also the second time it snowed that year in Lhasa. On the day of the first snowfall, she'd been filled with anxiety, and then those good-for-nothing kids had got her all worked up, putting her in an even fouler mood. Unlike the last time it snowed, she was feeling bright and cheery today. The snow was unremitting, but she had a nice warm fire going in the small room upstairs, where she was awaiting the arrival of an important guest. *Will he come? Of course he will. It's all been arranged. But will Drölkar come?*

She dialled Drölkar's number.

"Drölkar, you're definitely coming tonight? Like I said, I've got an important gentleman coming over and I want to introduce you. I think he'll be able to help get you a better job, one with better pay."

Drölkar hadn't really put much stock in what Butri had told her before, and if she hadn't received the phone call, she would have forgotten all about it. Now that Butri had called again, she felt she couldn't really refuse, so she told her she'd be over when she got off work.

A few days before, while Butri had been out buying meat at the Tromsikhang market, she had run into Karma Dorjé, an old customer of hers. "Mr. Karma-la!" she called out in a familiar tone. He looked around but acted as if he didn't recognize her. "Mr. Karma-la, so good to see you! It's me Butri, from Butri's Tibetan Cuisine. My, how forgetful you are! But I recognized you right away, standing out from the crowd like Venus in the night sky." As she spoke, she laid her package of meat on the ground. She gave her hands a perfunctory wipe on her *pangden* then held one out to him, which he shook reluctantly.

"Yes, yes. If you hadn't stopped me, I wouldn't have recognized you," he said as he inspected her from hatted head to shoed foot.

She stuck out her tongue a little, perhaps out of embarrassment or unease. "I've put on some weight, been drinking too much with the customers, and now… but business must be booming for you? Look how stout and glowing you are!" She chuntered on, trying to extricate herself from her awkwardness.

Karma Dorjé patted his sagging paunch. "You can't help but put on weight when you have to take clients to dinner every day. Can't do business on an empty stomach. But when women get fat they look like pigs. When it comes to women, they should have a body like that old saying: slim as bamboo from Tsari. That's what men like."

She flashed a fake smile and responded without missing a beat. "I know what type you like, sir. I've got a girl at the restaurant who's just come in from the country and she's right up your alley. You want looks, she's got looks, you want a figure, she's got a figure. You must come over and take a look." As soon as the words were out of her mouth, she was surprised by her own lie.

He chuckled dismissively. "A girl, you say? I didn't think Tibetan restaurants these days had any young girls left, just leftover noodles." Catching his implication, she gave him a playful shove, then put on her most fawning voice.

"If you don't believe me, sir, then I invite you to come and see for yourself this weekend. I guarantee you'll like what you see." That was how Karma Dorjé had ended up agreeing to come to Butri's restaurant.

Butri had told Karma Dorjé a lie bigger than a mountain. She had no idea where to find a girl like the one she'd described, but her purse wasn't exactly bulging at the moment, and she couldn't let go of her desire to see it once more overflowing with those scarlet hundred-yuan notes. Faces and bodies paraded through Butri's mind—all the young women she could think of who'd come from the country to the city to make money. And then she thought of Drölkar. Drölkar was from her hometown, and they were even distantly related. When she'd been short-staffed in the past, she'd tried to get Drölkar to come and help out at the restaurant, but the stubborn-willed girl had always refused. But this time she'd been absolutely adamant, and with no way to keep avoiding her, Drölkar had given in and agreed to come.

Drölkar arrived at the restaurant, wrapped up from head to toe, just as the fire in the stove had really got going. She'd been hoping to have a nice hot cup of tea on arrival, and maybe a bite to eat, but she was greeted with neither, only Butri staring at the clock on the wall.

"Drölkar, you're late! And just look at the state of you. Is this what a young lady should look like, all shabby and dishevelled? Go wash your face and brush your hair. He'll be here any minute." Butri, all in a fluster, grabbed her best clothes from the wardrobe and told Drölkar to go change.

Drölkar took in Butri's manic demeanour. "I was busy today, and it's cold, I didn't have time to wash my face. I can do it now. But what do I have to get changed for? Can't you get me a cup of tea and some hot food?" She went to wash her face. As Butri handed her a bottle of scented cleanser, she seized Drölkar's cracked hands and shook her head forlornly, a kind expression coming over her.

"We country folk have a tough lot in life. Just look at your hands. It pains my heart." She wiped the tears from her eyes and broke into a smile. "We might not be close, but we're from the same place, and we're still family, the same flesh and blood. I don't want to see you suffer. I want to find you a well-paid job, one that won't wear you out, and all of that will depend on you. I've got an important guest coming today. I want you to entertain him, to make sure his glass is always full and he's got someone to toast with. If he's pleased, you'll have it made, you'll be dining out on all the finest foods life has to offer!" Butri's expression turned to one of bliss, as though she were savouring some rare delicacy at that very moment.

Drölkar shook her head. "Achak, what are you talking about? I think you're mixed up—it sounds like you're the one who wants to eat all those fine foods. All I need is to make enough to put food on the table and set aside a little money here and there. Forget about those fancy delicacies—a steaming chunk of boiled yak meat, that's the height of luxury for me."

At that moment there came the sound of a man's voice from downstairs: "Is Butri here?" Butri responded immediately and hurriedly flung the bundle of clothes at Drölkar, jerking her head to the side to indicate the bathroom off in the corner where Drölkar should get changed. Butri bounded down the stairs to greet her guest, smoothing her hair as she went. Drölkar hadn't had any intention of changing her clothes, but having seen the way Butri was acting, she felt that this guest must be very important indeed and that she ought to look presentable for him. Reluctantly, she changed into the clothes that Butri had tossed at her.

"It's been such a long time since we've had the honour of your presence in my humble establishment, sir," said Butri, flashing her white teeth. "How wonderful that we ran into each other the other day! And you've brought a gentleman friend with you, too, I see. I'm so grateful that you're paying us a visit this evening." She ushered her guests upstairs. The arrival of the two men made Drölkar feel suddenly nervous and timid. She wanted nothing more than to get away, but it was too late now—there wasn't even a hole to hide her head in, let alone a means of escape. Out of options, she gently opened the door, emerged from the bathroom, and sat silently on the edge of the sofa.

Butri rushed to get down a crate of Pedrön.[1] "It's cold out today but I've got a nice fire going, so we'll pass on the hot drinks and get straight into the cold beer. As our honoured guests, I want you to make yourselves at home. My little sis over here will be joining us tonight to pour drinks and keep you company. She's just graduated middle school, she's a cultured girl and easy on the eye. She's been in school this whole time and hasn't met a lot of people out in the big wide world, so she gets a bit shy around people she doesn't know." As she spoke, she placed a can of beer in Drölkar's hands. All of a sudden, Drölkar had turned into a serving girl without quite knowing how—she wasn't sure if this was a dream or reality. Blushing deeply, her heart thumping wildly, she clutched the can of beer that Butri had forced into her hand and sat there at a loss. Butri gave her a subtle jab, indicating that she should pour drinks for the guests, and Drölkar snapped out of it. But as she was pouring their glasses, her hands were shaking so badly she spilt beer all over the table, covering it in froth.

Karma Dorjé found her clumsiness endearing, and without hesitation he grabbed Drölkar's cracked hands. "You're new, aren't you? Not to worry. Forget about the drinks for now. Why don't you come sit between us, you'll get used to it. Look at these hands! They look more like they're used to hard labour than holding a pen. But you've certainly got the type of looks a man likes." Karma Dorjé pulled Drölkar over and sat her between himself and the other man. She'd never been this close to a strange man before,

---

[1] Budweiser, that is—Lhasans give their beers women's names. Budweiser is Pedrön; Lhasa Beer is Lhakdrön.

much less been *with* a man, and her heart began to pound even harder. She broke out in a sweat; she could feel it beading on her palms and soaking her back. *What am I doing here? What am I playing at? This was a mistake...* Drölkar's mind raced with doubts, and she regretted having ever come.

After Butri had performed the first ceremonial toast to welcome her guests, she began to drink herself, and she also poured a small glass for Drölkar.

"What are you being so shy for? Have a drink and toast our guests."

"Don't put the girl on the spot," Karma Dorjé's companion said to Butri. "She's a novice, from the look of it. But she'll soon get used to it." Butri and the two men drank and talked idly about this, that, and the other: the news, the dealings of high officials, the goings on of friends, the lives of the common people.

When the sun set behind the hills to the west, the dice players downstairs stopped their game. They'd stuck around a bit longer that day, taking advantage of the nice warm fire, and they'd polished off a whole crate of Lhasa Beer. Now somewhat drunk, they staggered out the door, one after the other. Once she was sure they were gone, Butri poked her head out of the upstairs window and put on a fake smile. "Gentlemen, you're leaving? I'm afraid I have guests today so I can't see you off. The snow will still be around tomorrow and it'll probably be even colder than it was today, so you're welcome to come back here instead of freezing at home! I'll get the fire going early and wait for you." The old dice players waved a hand in response, indicating they'd be back tomorrow. Butri had in fact barely made an appearance all afternoon, only emerging to replenish their beer and settle the bill. Waving his hand in response, old Dawa muttered to the others, "Old Miss

Piggy really knows how to lay it on thick. The stars came out in the daytime, she gets a couple of new customers, then gives us the cold shoulder. If a new guest comes tomorrow, who knows if she'll light the stove for us? When you've got meat in hand, the vultures circle. Let's just see what kind of mood she's in when the sun comes up..." The other three men cackled in agreement with their companion's assessment, then they lumbered off their separate ways.

It was the old men's habit to come to the restaurant and while away the day with their games. When it came time to settle the bill, if they had to pull a hundred from their wallets, they would first scratch their bellies, then massage the note between their palms, so that by the time it got into Butri's hands it was a crumpled mess. Whenever they played their dice, the old-timers made a right old racket, and she couldn't stand the way they would lick their fingers and count the remaining hundreds in their wallets over and again when they lost a few tenners, as though they had just lost a thousand. And when the time came for them to pay up, there was another arduous performance. Compared to that, Butri would be dancing for joy and raking it in if she could get free-spending businessmen like Karma Dorjé in the door, the kind of bigshots who pulled scarlet hundreds out of their wallets without batting an eyelid. Of course Butri was going to give preferential treatment to customers like Karma Dorjé.

Butri had been waiting for the dice players to leave all day. Now that they were gone, she raced downstairs to shut up shop. "The old-timers have finally gone, thank god!" she announced as she came back upstairs. "And I've closed the restaurant for the night. This evening, we can all have a good drink together." As the night wore on, Butri kept filling their glasses and kept toasting her two guests.

The fire glowed brightly in the little iron stove and the small room was finally feeling warm and toasty. Butri and the two men had become flushed with the drink, while Drölkar was burning with anxiety, beads of sweat rolling down her forehead. She was starving, and she could hear her stomach growling with hunger. *What am I doing here? What's wrong with me, am I possessed?* She felt a deep pang of regret at having ever come, and worse, she had the ominous feeling that something terrible was about to happen to her.

The other three were all leaning in close, drinking and roaring and laughing. Karma Dorjé's roaming hands periodically pawed at Drölkar, groping their way over her body. She did her best to evade his lecherous advances. She was a grown woman now, but no man had ever put his hands on her like this. Karma Dorjé's touch revolted her; she tried to sit and endure it, but his hand, like the claw of some vile demon, kept on groping at her until Drölkar couldn't take it anymore. She leapt up from between the two men.

"Achak Butri, it's time for me to go home. I'm going home," she said, moving to leave.

Butri looked at her with two glittering drunken eyes and, grabbing her by the hand, sat her back down on the sofa. "Your Achak is a bit tipsy, surely you can't just leave us all like—like this? Besides, I've already locked the front door, so you're not going anywhere. In future you and I can run this place together, then you can give up on that hard labour. With a man like Mr. Karma Dorjé behind us our restaurant will do a roaring trade. Didn't I say I was having an important guest over today to discuss your future? Well the important guest, that's—that's him. When us country folk open a place in the city, we've got to rely on a man like him. So pour us some more drinks!"

Drölkar was incensed by this astonishing speech. Her expression darkened and her tone hardened. "Achak Butri, this is the reason you insisted I come here today? Well, if that's the case, I don't drink, and I don't know anything about hosting guests, either. Please unlock the door. I'm going home."

At this point, Karma Dorjé finally stirred from the sofa. "There's no need to put on an act, my darling," he said, patting the small of her back. "When country girls like you first come to the city you're all like this. But living in the big city isn't easy. Every little thing costs money—no one can get by without it. You're looking to survive, and we're looking for a good time. Now the little lamb's at the wolf's door, can the wolf just let it go without taking a bite of that soft flesh? So how about we just have a nice drink together and enjoy ourselves." He pressed a hand onto Drölkar's shoulder, forcing her back down onto the sofa. The implication of his words wasn't lost on her. There was no way out. Now Drölkar could do nothing but sit there, not daring to move a muscle, just like the little lamb at the wolf's door. Karma Dorjé picked up her glass, pressing her to drink. Drölkar squeezed her lips shut. But no matter how she twisted and turned, it was no use. Her first taste of beer was forced into her mouth. When the sharp, bitter liquid hit her throat, she felt a wave of nausea and almost threw up. Drölkar burst into a fit of coughing, but her reaction elicited no sympathy from the other three—on the contrary, they roared with laughter. This endeared her even further to Karma Dorjé. He pulled her roughly into his lap and pressed his stubbly, yellow-toothed mouth close to hers. "Good girl, have another drink," he said, forcing more beer into her mouth. "Beer is the best anaesthetic. It'll help you get over that shyness, then you can sing us a song. Booze was made for men to drink, songs were made for girls to sing."

"If you want a song, sing it yourself," Drölkar said, choking back tears. "I haven't had a thing to eat all day and I don't even have the strength to move. I beg you, please let me leave. Please."

Butri looked like these pleas had put her in a difficult position, and her words came out haltingly. "Where are you going to get something to eat at this hour? If you're hungry, drink some beer. It's made from grain—there's nothing more nutritious! You can get by on this stuff for days. Just look at your Achak—see how plump I got thanks to the amber nectar!" She had no intention of letting Drölkar go, and no intention of getting any food inside her, either.

Karma Dorjé rose and put on his coat. "It's alright, I'll go out and get the girl something to eat." But before he could leave, Butri hauled herself unsteadily off the sofa.

"This isn't a barren wasteland," she said. "It might not be gourmet, but I can rustle something up." She retrieved several flatbreads and a hunk of dried mutton from the cupboard. Drölkar was desperate to eat something, but she was even more desperate to escape. No matter how much they insisted, she wouldn't eat a bite. Without so much as touching the bread, the three drunks devoured the succulent mutton in the blink of an eye. The food seemed to sober them up a little, and they broke open a third crate of beer. The hands of the clock on the wall pointed to half past three, but they showed no signs of stopping. Drölkar wept, unable to take it anymore, but the others offered her no comfort and continued to ply her with drinks. She had no tolerance for alcohol, but they kept forcing her—Karma Dorjé even seized her neck and poured beer right into her mouth. No matter how Drölkar pleaded with them, it was no use. No matter how she tried to resist, she couldn't combat the persistence of all three of them.

They took turns pouring her drinks, and they continued to drink themselves, clinking an endless stream of toasts. They grew even more boisterous, the booze giving them a renewed energy.

Drölkar felt hot all over. Her head was pounding and the room was spinning—even the glasses and cans on the table were going in circles. When she saw them refilling the glasses once more, she felt a wave of nausea; pulling herself off the sofa, she staggered to the bathroom to throw up, but nothing came out of her empty stomach except for frothy liquid. She collapsed on the floor, unable to control her own body. Though she had no strength left, she was still thinking clearly, but she couldn't move when she tried to stand. Mustering all her effort, she picked herself up off the ground, staggered back into the room, and sat on the sofa. After some time, she fell into an exhausted sleep amid the noise of their chatter. Once she was out, there were some hushed discussions among Butri and her guests, after which the other man rose unsteadily to his feet on the pretence of going to relieve himself, and Butri jumped up quickly to help him downstairs. Time passed and no one came back; not even a bump or a sound from below—all was quiet. The fire in the stove was still burning bright, and the water in the kettle on top had almost all boiled away. Only Karma Dorjé and Drölkar remained in the little room. The unusual quiet roused Drölkar from her sleep, and when she saw the scene before her she panicked. Lurching to her feet, she grabbed the door handle in an attempt to escape, but the door had been locked from the outside. She yanked it fiercely, but it wouldn't budge. Her terror rising, Drölkar called out for Butri, but no one answered. At that moment Karma Dorjé rose from the couch and grabbed Drölkar's hand.

"Poor girl. Hush now. You can shout yourself hoarse, but no

one's coming. If there's some money in it for your Achak Butri, innocent country girls like you end up locked upstairs. You were brought here today just for me, and I'm not paying for nothing." The burly Karma Dorjé dragged Drölkar into his lap as though he were picking up a baby bird.

Outside, the snow was gently falling. On that silent night, when the whole city seemed like it had fallen into a deep sleep, the wolves and jackals had conspired against her. Drölkar's mind was fuzzy, and as she lost the strength to fight back, Karma Dorjé pressed his full weight on top of her. She was drunk and everything had grown hazy, but she knew exactly what was happening to her. Her heart pounded wildly. "Let me go," she pleaded weakly as she tried with all her might to fend him off, but her body was so numbed from the alcohol she could barely lift her hands. In the face of Karma Dorjé's power and brutality, she was as helpless as a child.

Karma Dorjé stole the flower of Drölkar's youth on that dense snowy night, without pity or compassion. From that moment on, her pure, untouched body had been forever tarnished, stained like the clean white snow on which Butri had thrown a black lump of coal on the day of the first snowfall.

The next day, the merciful sun rose slowly over the mountains in the east. The sun was bright and blazing as always, but that day it seemed cold and indifferent. Sunlight gradually penetrated the windows of the little room. The floor was covered in beer cans and one half-full glass still sat on the table—the others were in pieces on the floor. Drölkar had thrown them at Karma Dorjé the night before in an effort to defend herself. She was no match for him, and the glasses ended up smashed on the ground, shards scattered among the beer cans.

"First comes the snow, cool and white, then comes the sun, nice and warm." Just as the folk song goes, the sun was shining brightly in the sky that morning, but Drölkar felt no warmth when its rays touched her body. It was unclear when the blazing fire from the night before had died out, and the leftover mutton bones sat on the table, mocking her. Her body was frozen stiff and her eyes were puffed up and red from crying. When she looked out of the window with those swollen eyes, she saw the snow melting on the eaves, falling drip by drip into the alley below. She gathered her senses and tried to get up, but all at once she was mentally and physically assailed by feelings of anger, shame, despair, sorrow, hunger, and thirst. She couldn't move a muscle, let alone stand. Overcome with anguish, she burst into tears. The sound was so heartbreaking that anyone who heard it would be moved to tears as well, but the lifeless little room remained unmoved. She wept for an age, until no more tears came, as though her eyes had run completely dry.

Tak, tak—she heard someone coming up the stairs. Butri entered bearing a thermos of sweet tea and a steaming bowl of noodles. The room was so littered with beer cans and carboard boxes there wasn't a place to put the thermos down. Butri swept the cans and shards of glass to one side. She sighed deeply, remorse etched onto her face, and moved to touch Drölkar's numbed hands. But Drölkar, who a moment ago had been lying there paralyzed, suddenly leapt at her like a fierce tigress, slapping her in the face.

"You monster! Why didn't you let me go? We might not love each other like family—but how could you be so cruel?" Her words came out like the howl of a wild animal.

Butri didn't say anything at first, she simply sat on the edge of the bed and inhaled a fingernail of snuff. Tears falling from her eyes, she spoke softly. "Drölkar, if hitting me makes you feel better, then go ahead. When us poor country girls come to the city, we fall in love with the bright lights and the last thing we want is to go back home. I had to keep living somehow, I had no choice. When you're hurting, you can lay your burdens on me. But when I was working as a maid and the man of the house took advantage of me, there was no one I could turn to, I had to keep the shame deep down inside. I lived that wretched life for a long time, terrified that his wife would find out. In the end, she did. She called me a slut, said I'd seduced her husband, and I lost my whole five-years' worth of wages. I was driven out of there with nothing but the clothes on my back."

When Butri had finished speaking, she sighed deeply. She poured the tea into a cup and handed it to Drölkar. "I know you're unhappy. We're from the same place, you and me, we share the same blood, and I want things to be better for you than they are now. What people like that bastard Karma Dorjé have is money. What you have is youth and your looks. If you really think about it, that kind of work isn't all that hard. There's lots of people in the city doing it these days, both openly and on the sly. The two of us can save up a bit of money together, and when we've got enough, we can buy a little place in the city, and we can use what's left to open a little business. Wouldn't that be a better life than working our fingers to the bone in the countryside, sweating and toiling three hundred and sixty days a year?" She poured out all her plans to Drölkar, holding nothing back.

The day that Butri's former employers drove her out the door, she bit her lip and vowed that she would never be separated from the wonderful city of Lhasa. She rented a cheap place on the outskirts of town and started looking for suitable work, but nothing came along. She ended up doing what the Chinese migrant workers did:

shouldering a huge plastic sack, she spent her mornings going from school to school, scrambling around with the beggar children to collect cans. After that she would head to the most popular pilgrimage circuits—the Tsekhor, the Barkhor, the Lingkhor—wherever the most people were to be found, that's where she went. When the sack was full, she sold the contents to a Chinese waste collector, and for a long time, this was how she made enough to eat and pay her fifty yuan rent. That sort of scrap metal fetched a better price back then, so with the little extra money she made from selling cans she went to the Tromsikhang market and picked up some odds and ends, which she then sold on the Barkhor in the evening. And that was how, bit by bit, she finally saved enough to open her restaurant.

Hearing Butri's story aroused some sympathy in Drölkar, but she still didn't say anything. *Why did you pass on the pain to me instead of getting even with those who wronged you,* she thought to herself. She shut her eyes tightly and once again shed bitter tears of grief. *My body was a precious gift given to me by my parents and I couldn't look after it. What possessed me to listen to this monster? Now I've been sucked into a swamp and everything is finished, it's all over. I could scratch the skin right off her face but it wouldn't make my body clean again. I must have done something terrible in a past life for this to be my punishment. What can I do now but accept my fate? All I have left now is a tormented heart, a tainted body, and tears that will never dry up.*

She rose slowly and moved unsteadily towards the stairs. Butri jumped up and seized her hand. "Drölkar, please don't leave like this. We have to sell our youth to survive, what other choice do we have..."

Before she'd finished, Drölkar wheeled around and looked right into her pleading face with eyes turned red from rage. "You think everyone's like you? Those rapists can take our possessions, our rights, even our lives, but your pride belongs to you alone, and no one can ever take that." With that, she left.

The snowy white alleys were still the same as the day before, but the girl walking through them was no longer the pure and innocent Drölkar of yesterday. Her lips were parched and her mouth was gummy. She wasn't crying now. She didn't have the energy anymore. She dragged her weary limbs through the streets, going nowhere in particular. Every time the dreamlike events of the night before came to her mind, her body trembled and her pounding little heart almost split into pieces. She thought of her mother, and she thought of her snowy mountain home. She was suddenly overcome, body and soul, with an intense desire to go back home, back to the place she was born and raised.

Two

1

From the day that she walked out of Butri's restaurant, Drölkar cut off all ties to her family and everyone close to her. Back in her village, everyone had their own version of what had happened to Drölkar, but initially her parents had clung to the belief that she'd gone off to find a job somewhere, and they continued to wait and hope that she'd soon return home. Time marched unstoppably forward; days, months, years passed, but still they heard nothing of their daughter. Yangdzom, Drölkar's close friend, had likewise disappeared, leaving as much trace as a rainbow. At first Drölkar's younger brother, Tsering, had believed the letters he eventually received from his sister and was entirely convinced that she had moved somewhere to find a job. He missed his sister from the bottom of his heart, but he took all his emotions and poured them into his studies. His tireless dedication bore fruit and he was rewarded with outstanding grades, and after he graduated, he was assigned a job in Lhasa.

Through all those years, he was never able to put his sister out of his mind. Whenever he had any good news, she was always the first person he wanted to share it with, and whenever he was feeling down, he missed her even more. Now that he had a regular salary, he felt it was time to repay his sister for everything she had done for him. She was in his thoughts day and night, but he couldn't even catch sight of her shadow, let alone Drölkar herself. Nevertheless, he clung steadfast to the notion of tracking her down, and whenever he had time in amongst his daily business, he was posting missing persons ads to the newspapers and the local TV station. He wasn't like his extremely devout parents, but as soon as he got off work he went to circumambulate the Barkhor along with all the city's old and faithful, just to look for his sister.

Now, making his way round the Barkhor three times a day had almost become an obligatory task. The crowds at the Barkhor were huge. They grew in size as the sun began to set and reached their peak with the onset of dusk. The old folks intoned their *manis* and plied their prayer beads, rushing heedlessly onwards, paying not the slightest attention to the people around them. Some of the younger people munched on fried dough and glanced into the shops as they went around, while others engaged in carefree chit-chat.

Tsering wasn't to be found in any of their ranks. Unlike the other circumambulators, not one syllable of a *mani* passed his lips and no prayer beads were clutched in his hands. Nor did he have any fellow pilgrims he could shoot the breeze with. Among the crowds of the Barkhor, he was always making his way slowly and deliberately, completely alone. He got into the habit of scanning the crowd with alert eyes, paying particular attention to the young women. As he walked, he scrutinized each and every one, not letting a single face escape his attention.

That day, as usual, he headed to the Barkhor when he got off work. He noticed a young woman in the crowd that looked like his sister. He watched her from afar, not daring to get too close. The more he looked, the more he felt she resembled her. He kept following, and, unable to help himself, tugged her gently from behind and called out to her: "Sister." The woman looked him up and down, then brushed him off irritably. "Creep!" she spat, giving him a look of utter contempt. Her companion, too, looked at him askance and said, "Ignore him. He must have a screw loose." With a burst of contemptuous laughter, they walked off.

Tsering learned his lesson. After that experience, he kept his distance whenever he saw a young woman that looked like his sister, eyeing them from the front, the back, and the side. Every single time he ended up shaking his head in disappointment and returning home, sighing to himself.

People from their village said all sorts of things about what had become of Drölkar. Some said she'd gone to work in construction, and unable to bear the demands of physical labour, she'd fled to India. Some said she'd been married off to a Hui Muslim trader and had moved to some corner of Gansu, and now she was stuck there with no way to get home. Some said she'd gone to Lhasa, where she made a living as a waitress at a Tibetan restaurant, all tarted up with make-up, flashy clothes, and a fancy hairdo. Still others said that she'd been duped by a Chinese human trafficker, who'd sold her somewhere off in China. Every man and woman had their own version of the story, and each story was told with breathless certainty and in minute detail, as though the person had seen it all with their own eyes.

At first, their little village was all abuzz with talk of Drölkar's disappearance, but with the passage of time, fewer and fewer people spoke of her. Now, when young women left the village and moved to the city to make some money, their parents would say, "You've got to be smart when you're away from home. Don't go vanishing without a trace like that Drölkar. No matter how nice it is elsewhere, home is where the heart is, and it's the place you'll always come back to. Don't get taken in by the Chinese or the Hui Muslims, and make sure you bring yourself back." In this way,

Drölkar became a cautionary tale for all the young girls from the village who went off to the city to find work. Apart from that, pretty much no one mentioned her anymore.

Time moved on, and the outside world continued to change with it, but there was no way Drölkar's parents could forget about their daughter—their own flesh and blood. In fact, the passage of time just made them feel her absence all the more acutely. In the beginning, all the gossip and rumours had meant that Drölkar was never out of their thoughts; now that the rumours had died down and no one spoke of her, they thought of their daughter even more.

After that year's busy spring work in the fields had passed, Tsering phoned his parents and, at his suggestion, they came to Lhasa, where they could visit the holy sites while they clung to the faintest of hopes and continued to look for their beloved Drölkar.

It was the 15th day of the Saga Dawa Festival, which happened to fall on Tsering's day off, and at his parents' request he set out early to take them to the Lingkhor. It was hot during the month of Saga Dawa, but it seemed like rain always came on the morning of the 15th, whether light or heavy. That year, however, had been especially dry, and no rain fell that morning like it normally did. The Lingkhor route was packed and there were countless people making smoke offerings, blanketing the whole of the city in the sweet scent of incense. The smoke hung over Lhasa's bright dawn streetlights like a thick fog, turning them hazy. Far from masking Lhasa's charm, this simply lent the city an even greater air of serenity.

There were so many people on the Lingkhor and the streets were so narrow that it almost felt like every house in the city had been emptied out. The normally nimble Ama Pedrön, Tsering's mother, walked with difficulty, as though her legs had been put in shackles. As a country woman, she felt that she couldn't compete with these brazen, self-centred city folks, so she ceded the road to them, letting people past one after another. Tsering's frail father was unused to the crowds and he had a headache that day, so he could only manage to shuffle along slowly. The other pilgrims on the route came rushing straight past them, their sense of urgency and their ostentatiously large strides seeming to convey a message: *This is one of the most important festivals of the year, commemorating the enlightenment and passage into nirvana of our Lord Buddha, and today, more than any other day, we need to do our prostrations and circumambulations! After the Lingkhor we need to circle the Potala Palace on the Tsekhor, and then there's still the Barkhor to do—so get out of the way!*

2

THOUGH TSERING AND HIS PARENTS LEFT HOME AT SIX O'CLOCK in the morning, the sun was already up by the time they made it to the Thousand Buddhas. There, on the southern face of Chakpo Hill, stands a large carving of the Buddha. Since the 1990s, the people of Lhasa have taken to calling it the Thousand Buddhas on account of the many smaller carvings that surrounded the main image. Such images are the most sacred form of representation of the Buddha and are the main object of a Buddhist's faith. Of all the different figures depicted in Buddhism, the image of the Buddha reigns supreme and always occupies pride of place, be it in a household shrine or the altar of a temple. The pilgrims on the Lingkhor prostrated themselves and prayed before the Thousand Buddhas, and most of them went to a teahouse to relax over a cup of sweet tea and a bowl of noodles when they were done with their worship. When Tsering and his parents arrived at the Thousand Buddhas, his mum and dad were overcome with feelings of reverence and fell to a lengthy spell of prayers and prostrations. Only when they were finished did they notice their hunger and thirst, at which point Tsering took them to a nearby place called the "Pilgrims Teahouse."

The teahouse was so crowded there was barely a space to stand, let alone a free seat. The chatter of the customers filled the whole place with noise. Tsering's mother wrinkled her nose in disapproval and turned to her son, looking thoroughly fed up. "Let's go home, son. That's the city for you—such big crowds. Wherever you go there's nothing but people. Your dad and I aren't used to all this hubbub and we both feel a headache coming on." Tsering looked at his mother and replied patiently, "Mum, let's get a cup of tea and something to eat. We're only halfway round the route. We have to light some butter lamps as well, which'll take some time."

He scoured the teahouse, looking for somewhere to sit, and after a little while a spot opened up in the back. Making their way through the crowds, the three of them installed themselves in the open nook. A waitress came and gave the table a cursory wipe with a dirty rag before barking at them impatiently.

"What're you having? We're busy today so if you're not quick about it, your food won't be either."

"We'll have a thermos of sweet tea and three bowls of noodles," Tsering replied.

Their food arrived in short order, but his parents left the noodles completely untouched, having nothing but a couple of cups of tea. "Eat some noodles. There's nothing to eat back at home," Tsering said, but his mother shook her head.

"If you go around eating any old thing in the city, it's not just the disgusting smell you have to put up with. The food isn't clean—eating it would make my teeth hurt."

His father agreed. "Your mother's right, son," he said, taking some fried dough cakes from his bag that he'd brought from home, which he divided up to serve as their breakfast. His parents' refusal to eat a proper breakfast concerned Tsering and he lost his appetite, but he forced himself to eat since the noodles were already there. Not wanting to leave the rest, he packed up the leftover noodles and they exited the bustling teahouse. Outside, an elderly beggar was sitting by the doorway, his hands outstretched, loudly intoning the *Barché Lamsel*: "Dispel the outer obstacles externally, dispel the inner obstacles internally, dispel the secret obstacles into space. In devotion, I prostrate and take refuge in you." Tsering went to give the man his leftovers, but the beggar recoiled with a pained expression. "Kind sir, the layfolk of Lhasa are a generous lot, especially the kind-hearted people on the Lingkhor, so I am already full and quenched of thirst. But I am an old man with many aches and pains. Perhaps you, kind sir, could spare some change?" Tsering thought the old man's performance was over the top. He declined to give him any money, and even took the change he already had in his palm, originally meant as alms for the beggars, and stuffed it back in his pocket. Acting as though he hadn't heard the old man, Tsering went on his way without a backward glance.

They had planned to head over to the Thousand Buddhas to light butter lamps, but when they arrived there was a crowd of people gathered off to the side of the road looking at something. They went to see what was going on, and it turned out to be a fortune teller performing dice divinations. The onlookers were discussing the man's prowess in tones of amazement; among them there was one particularly vocal woman who plied her prayer beads incessantly as she spoke: "Last year I lost a necklace made from pure turquoise and coral. I looked for it everywhere but couldn't find it. I always have a lot of guests coming by my house, so at the time I thought someone must have taken it by mistake and I gave up hope. But that lovely necklace was so dear to me, and I just couldn't put it out of my mind. One day, when I was walking the Lingkhor, there was a big crowd of people gathering round this man asking him to tell their fortunes. I wasn't really hoping for anything, but I asked him to find out what had happened to my necklace all the same, and he answered me with complete confidence. 'The necklace never left your house,' he said. 'Go home, seek to the north, and you are sure to find it.' I wasn't really convinced, as I'd looked everywhere I could think of at home with no luck. I knew there was no hope, but the next morning I looked again anyway, combing through every nook and cranny on the north end of my house. Still there was no sign of my necklace. I'd looked everywhere but down the back of the cabinet, so for peace of mind I pulled it out a bit and there was my precious necklace right before my eyes, all covered in dust! The man's a Buddha in the flesh." When they heard this, Drölkar's parents snapped to attention, and it was as if their headaches and their distaste for the crowds had disappeared all of a sudden. Their eyes wide and their ears pricked up, they hung on the woman's every word, nodding their heads vigorously. It was as if they had found a powerful saviour, and they were filled with the hope that their daughter Drölkar—just like that necklace—would magically spring from the ground or drop from the sky.

They seemed to feel shy about asking the fortune teller about Drölkar, or perhaps they felt that it wasn't appropriate to do it in front of the crowd, and so they waited until he had finished with everyone else.

Two years before, when people from the village had asked

about their daughter Drölkar, they always proudly replied that she'd moved to Lhasa to work at some big company. Two years later, whenever anyone spoke about their daughter, they simply changed the subject. Before the Tibetan New Year, when they saw all those people coming home from the city to celebrate Losar, laden with gifts and their wallets bulging, Drölkar's parents felt as though they'd been stabbed in the heart. They'd waited and waited, thinking that they wouldn't mind if Drölkar came back empty handed—they just wanted her home. But now they couldn't find a trace of their daughter. They had no idea where she'd gone—they didn't even know if she was alive or dead—and it felt like their hearts were being shredded. Now, her parents' whole world had been cloaked in darkness; even in the daytime they largely shut themselves up at home, and if they didn't have anything important to do, they couldn't bring themselves to go outside at all.

At Losar, the villagers gathered in the evening to sing and perform the circle dance. In years past, Ama Pedrön had always been very fond of the festivities—in fact she was one of the lead dancers and singers. But with the disappearance of her daughter, her enthusiasm for such things had evaporated.

When the other villagers went to plant prayer flags on the third day of Losar, Ama Pedrön and her husband did not accompany them, instead setting out early in the morning to make offerings at the mountaintop. In the afternoon they continued to avoid the others by going down to the river, where they prayed desperately to be reunited with their daughter. This behaviour sparked a great deal of talk among the villagers, and some of them, paying close attention to the old couple's expressions, determined that some tragedy must have befallen Drölkar. After a tragedy comes a time when the sadness fades, and after a death comes a time when you get over the grief. But it seemed as though there never did come a time when the darkness lifted from their home, when the pain went away.

The fortune teller's customers eventually dispersed, and the father, Tsewang, placed a fifty yuan note inside a *khata* scarf, which he laid at the diviner's feet. "Sir, we beg of you…" said Tsewang, kneeling before him. The fortune teller offered no response; he simply sat there inspecting them and chanting his *manis*.

Ama Pedrön's eyes were tinged with sadness, Tsering's expression was one of hopelessness, and Tsewang's despairing gaze was fixed on the fortune teller imploringly. It was obvious to the fortune teller from the looks on their faces that they were suffering. "*Om mani padme hum,*" he said, "there is never any happiness on the needle-tip of samsara. *Ya.* What can I help you with?"

Tsewang clasped his palms to his chest and issued a long, despondent sigh. "It's my daughter, sir. She came to Lhasa two years ago looking for work and we haven't seen her since. Now we don't know if she's dead or alive. We've searched high and low but haven't found a trace of her. We've asked everyone we can think of, but we've had no news at all."

"What is her zodiac sign?" asked the fortune teller, gathering his prayer beads.

Tsewang felt a fresh wave of hope. "She's a rabbit, she'd be twenty-two this year."

The fortune teller intoned something unintelligible, rubbed his dice, and cast them into the cup. Though he didn't show them the result, the sharp-eyed Tsering saw that it was three fours—twelve. The fortune teller shook the dice again, and once more three fours came out. He shook his head slightly and took the three dice in his hand, blew on them, and cast them back into the cup. This time it was two fives and a two—twelve again. The fortune teller snapped up the dice in a flash to hide the result, but Tsering had seen the three rolls clear as day, and moreover he had seen the words in the fortune teller's book: "An extremely ill omen." He was worried: what did it mean, three twelves in a row?

The fortune teller closed his divination manual and said, "Old sir, I'm afraid this does not augur well—it will be most difficult to find your daughter. These days there are so many young women coming from the country to find work then disappearing without a trace. What is the cause of all this? I'm afraid I do not know. But this mundane world is one of samsaric existence, and always will it be so. I will say this: it is indeed true that all compound phenomena are impermanent and all that is corrupt is suffering. Cyclical existence is impermanent and humans, like unconditioned space, cannot exist forever. Therefore, you should not seek your daughter from now on. It is likely that she has found her own path that she now walks upon. There is no use in suffering further; dedicate yourselves instead to prayer and worship. The flowers of our Snowlands' inhabitants have been blessed by the divine fortune of the noble Avalokiteśvara and the Dharma fortune of the six-syllable mantra, therefore you must apply yourself to the recitation of *manis*, cultivating compassion in this life and protecting yourself from suffering in the lower realms of existence in the next. There is nothing greater than this profound Dharma. In the beginning there is no difficulty in learning, in the middle there is no pride in knowledge, in the end there is no fear of forgetting. If it is like this, it will be beneficial both for this life and the next." After concluding his lavish speech, the fortune teller dipped his fingers into a vessel and sprinkled them with consecrated water.

Tsering's parents didn't really grasp what the fortune teller had said, but they still understood that there was no hope for finding their daughter. They weren't at all taken aback to hear this now, as they'd been searching for Drölkar for a long time; they were tired, they had sunk into a boundless sea of suffering from which there was no escape, and any slender hope they once had was now all but extinguished. They received the consecrated water in their cupped palms, drank some, requested blessings, then rubbed the water on their heads and around their eyes. The fortune teller took a package from a cardboard box, extracted some pills that he wrapped in a sheet of paper, then he pressed them into Ama Pedrön's hands. "These are *mani* pills that have been blessed by holy men from both India and Tibet. They have the power to vanquish the undesirable pains of sentient beings and to extend one's lifespan. Take one on the morning of holy days. *Om mani padme hum.*" The three of them felt as though they still had questions for the fortune teller, yet without asking a thing they thanked him profusely and went on their way. From then on, it was as if there had been an announcement that Drölkar no longer remained in this world. After hearing the fortune teller's words, it was as though their sorrow had reached its limit and the hope of seeing their daughter again, accumulated over days and months of waiting, had suddenly diminished.

Whether Drölkar was still in this world or was on the path to the next, she would always be in their hearts. They offered a thousand butter lamps before the Thousand Buddhas, and Tsewang, with great effort, brought his ailing limbs to the floor to prostrate seven times before the great image of the Buddha. "Gods, lamas, dakinis, wise dharma protectors, guardian deities," he said, clasping his palms to his chest, "Having your flesh and blood child die before her parents is something I wouldn't wish on my worst enemies. I still don't know if my poor daughter is alive or dead, but if she's no longer with us, please take her quickly to a good rebirth. If she is still alive, I beg you to bring her home to her parents as soon as possible." He couldn't stop the tears rolling down his cheeks, and he turned to the side, pretending to pray so that his wife and son wouldn't see. Ama Pedrön touched her prayer beads to her forehead and focused her attention on the face of the Buddha as her quivering lips murmured a prayer. No one could hear what Ama Pedrön was saying to the towering figure, but she was surely pouring out the pain and grief of missing her beloved daughter and entreating him to reunite them as soon as possible. Tsering offered a butter lamp and lit a stick of incense. With his hands clasped, he focused single-mindedly on his prayer: "Precious One, I don't care if it's good or bad, just please bring us news of my dear sister as soon as possible."

Three

1

MANY GIRLS FROM THE COUNTRY COME TO THE CITY TO work as housemaids or to make money doing other odd jobs. Yangdzom was from the same village as Drölkar, and she had likewise found herself moving to the city, where she took a job as a maid. That year, Yangdzom was just a child of thirteen. She had been brought from the country to serve in the Lhasa residence of a county official named Nyendrak, an arrangement that had been arrived at after consultations between Nyendrak, the village head, and Yangdzom's grandparents. Nyendrak's work kept him away in the county, so most of the time the only people at home were his wife, Achak Drölma, and his daughter.

Their house was large, two stories. It was a beautiful place: impeccably designed, with a spacious courtyard and well-lit rooms that were filled with sunlight from the moment the sun rose over the eastern mountains to the moment it set in the west. On the first day Yangdzom arrived, Achak Drölma, the lady of the house, made her wash from head to toe, then she threw Yangdzom's *chuba* and other old clothes into a sack, which she tied tightly and placed outside on the veranda. She retrieved some old items from the wardrobe which belonged to her daughter, Tenzin Lhadzé, and had Yangdzom put them on.

The clothes make the woman, indeed. This coarse country girl was now adorned with a clean and modern outfit. Her hair, done up in a braid, hung down her back and she looked every bit a genuine city girl. It seemed to dawn on her now that the only real difference between city and country folk was in fact their clothes. That night, Ms. Drölma made up a place for Yangdzom to sleep in the kitchen. Yangdzom didn't mind this at all, since their kitchen was even cleaner than the little shrine room at Yangdzom's family home. When Ms. Drölma entered her "bedroom," she already felt as though the little room was her own private world. When the lady of the house left and she was alone in the kitchen, Yangdzom ran her finger over the windowsills and the table and found that everything was absolutely spotless. Even more incredible to her was that she could see her face in the white tiles on the walls, as clear as if she was looking in a mirror. To her amazement, she discovered that the woman in those white tiles no longer had grubby, unkempt plaits; now she looked like one of those young women who worked at the county government, the only difference being that they did their hair up with clips and bobby pins whereas hers was in a braid. The more she looked at the reflection of this woman wearing fetching modern clothes, the more she began to doubt that it was herself. She touched her hands to her cheeks—this was no dream, it was reality. She covered her face, too embarrassed to keep looking. *Will I be a city girl from now on?* She climbed into bed, but her mind was racing. She spent her first night in the city sleeplessly, her head filled with thoughts of the past and fantasies of the future.

In days gone by, she'd always felt that the night went by in a heartbeat; today, she finally discovered just how long that time between dusk and dawn could be. By daybreak she was sleeping softly, but not long after the kitchen door opened with a bang. For a moment she was unsure of where she was, and then it came back to her. She jumped out of bed in a fluster as she offered her apologies to the mistress. "I'm so sorry, Miss. I was out like a light."

"In future you must take care of all the household duties," Ms. Drölma replied as she got the butter tea ready. "But this time you can watch me and learn how to make the tea and prepare breakfast."

Achak Drölma cut off a huge hunk of butter from the block and dropped it nonchalantly in the tea churn. Yangdzom was stunned, thinking to herself that if she used such an enormous slab at home, she'd be using up a week's worth of butter for the whole family in one go. "Yangdzom, pay close attention to how I perform the household duties," Achak Drölma said as she made the tea. "I don't want to have to show you a second time. We are a small family and we place importance on clean, healthy food. In the country it's all about quantity, but here in the city, we value flavour, presentation, and fragrance above all. You must keep this in mind. We had a cleaner come every week in the past since our house is so large, but from now on that will be your job. You must clean the house inside and out. But you don't need to do much today. Tomorrow morning you will go to the hospital to have a check-up." She spoke authoritatively, like a supervisor delegating tasks to her employees.

Yangdzom replied deferentially, but with puzzlement. "Yes, Miss, I'll remember everything you said. But, Miss, I'm not sick, so why do I need to go the hospital?"

"This you do not understand. It's called a physical. It costs a lot of money. Having a full-body check-up is beneficial for you, too."

"But I'm not sick, so why do I need to go to the hospital?" Yangdzom asked again, insistent.

"You will understand later," Ms. Drölma replied solemnly. "First do as I say. It will be good for you."

Yangdzom still didn't understand why she had to go to the hospital when there was nothing wrong with her. Her head was full of questions, but she felt that she shouldn't badger the mistress, so she grabbed the broom and went to sweep the courtyard.

At breakfast, Tenzin Lhadzé downed a cup of tea without even sitting, then set off for school munching on a spongy hunk of flatbread. Ms. Drölma was the same: she simply ate a bit of tsampa then rushed off to work, and Mr. Nyendrak likewise went on his way. Yangdzom was left in the huge house with just the dog, Cub, for company, and everything felt incredibly still and quiet.

Having been plunged so suddenly into such an unfamiliar environment, everything seemed surreal to her. Though the mistress had set out her tasks, Yangdzom had no idea where to begin. She went upstairs clutching a cleaning cloth, then came back downstairs and fetched the broom again, which passed a bit of time.

Before she'd left that morning, Ms. Drölma had said to her, "My daughter and I shan't be home for lunch today, and Nyendrak will be out as well. You and Cub may eat as you see fit." After they left, Yangdzom ate a flatbread from the plate, and for Cub she tore up a dried chunk of steamed bread, but he simply sat there barking and staring at her, not taking a bite. She looked at the puppy imploringly. "Come on Cub, eat up. The two of us'll be spending a lot of time together from now on, so you should eat what I give you!" The little dog simply stared at her wide-eyed and barked even louder, still showing no intention of touching the food. "Fine, it's your loss," she said, giving him the stink-eye. She roamed the house upstairs and down clutching her broom, but found herself unable to clean anything.

That afternoon, Ms. Drölma returned home punctually. For the evening meal, Drölma reheated the leftover vegetables from the day before and bought some steamed rolls from the place next door, and the two of them ate together. Shortly after they'd finished, Ms. Drölma turned to Yangdzom and issued a firm statement. "Get an early night tonight. You must go to the hospital for your check-up tomorrow, so be sure to rest well. Do not drink anything before your appointment. You may have breakfast after it's done." Yangdzom still wanted to ask why she needed to go to the hospital when nothing was wrong with her, but she swallowed her words when she saw Ms. Drölma's stern expression. She fell asleep instantly that night, so she had no idea what time Nyendrak and Lhadzé came home.

Yangdzom got up early the next day, as the mistress had ordered. She washed then went to sweep the yard. After that, she fetched a cloth and wiped the stove and the tables—even though they were already spotless—then awaited further instructions from the mistress.

Nyendrak had set off early that morning as he had to return to the county. He left without anyone seeing him off and without having so much as a hot cup of tea. This made Yangdzom feel rather uneasy, but she had only just arrived and didn't know what to do about it. Shortly after Nyendrak left, Ms. Drölma rose, went to the bathroom, then spent almost half an hour sitting in front of the vanity doing her makeup. Yangdzom could see all this through the kitchen window, and she was amazed by just how long people in the city took to get ready.

Ms. Drölma finally emerged from the bathroom some thirty minutes later, and, as she had the previous morning, made a large pot of tea. She ate only half a flatbread with her tea, then she jumped to her feet, disappeared into another room, and emerged clutching a pretty little handbag.

"Let's go to the hospital," she said.

"Please, Miss, have your breakfast first. Don't mind me," Yangdzom replied with concern.

Achak Drölma gave her a funny look. "*Ah tsi*, what an odd one you are. My stomach is my own business." This was the first reprimand that Yangdzom had received since coming to the city.

Yangdzom followed Ms. Drölma, immersed in her own thoughts. That morning, after a few beeps of the alarm clock, Lhadzé had rushed out of bed, rushed in and out of the bathroom, and then left for school with nothing but a cup of tea inside her. *Incredible—are city people's stomachs smaller than ours or something?* Her dear departed mother was right: the only thing I felt in Lhasa was hunger, she'd once told her. *I'll have to watch how much I eat from now on.* She fixed her gaze on Ms. Drölma's back as she turned over these problems in her mind, and soon they arrived at the hospital. It was the biggest hospital she'd ever seen. Everywhere she looked there were crowds of people: patients, nurses, doctors, people collecting prescriptions, people taking numbers; every available nook and cranny in the place—north, south, east, and west—was a hive of activity. Yangdzom gaped at all the people before her, wondering in amazement where they had all come from.

Ms. Drölma led her through the hospital corridors, obviously very familiar with the place. She entered a small room and then emerged with a Chinese doctor who wore a white coat and glasses. From there they headed for the second floor as Ms. Drölma and the doctor spoke in Chinese, which Yangdzom only half understood. There was a great crowd of patients waiting up on the second floor, but Ms. Drölma and the doctor forced straight through the middle of them and into another room, Yangdzom in tow. The Chinese doctor with the white coat and glasses whispered some words into the ear of another doctor who was in the room, and with a practiced hand she immediately drew a vial of blood from Yangdzom's arm. Ms. Drölma and Yangdzom went back downstairs. After passing through several brightly lit corridors, she was led into a dark room. The doctor pressed some cold metal or glass object to her chest, went into another room, then spoke to her through a window with some poorly pronounced Tibetan: "Breathe in… and hold…" She did as the doctor said, and her examination was over.

When they got home, Ms. Drölma took a dainty little cup from the cupboard and filled it with tea. The big china mug that Nyendrak had given to Yangdzom the day before was nowhere to be seen. She thought back to that morning when she had been cleaning in the kitchen. Nyendrak had just walked out the door, setting off for the county, but a moment later he'd re-entered and come into the kitchen with some advice. "My dear," he said, "this is your home. Don't be shy about eating your fill. If you don't, well, no one here's going to encourage you to eat, like they do in the country." But the teacup that Ms. Drölma gave to her now was even smaller than the one they'd used on the altar back home. Thinking about that little offering cup in turn aroused memories of her late parents, and she felt suddenly downcast. Ms. Drölma had no idea what was on Yangdzom's mind, and even if she knew, she still wouldn't give her a bigger cup. Ms. Drölma put the plate of leftover bread in front of Yangdzom. "Eat. For the next few days your cleaning duties will suffice. You do not need to take charge of the cooking yet, but pay close attention to how I do it. In the future, you will be responsible for all these tasks." This was what she'd said before, but the truth of the matter was that she didn't want Yangdzom making their food before the test results came back. And so, Yangdzom spent the next three days sweeping, dusting, and mopping. When it came time to cook, she helped wash the vegetables and watched how Ms. Drölma prepared the food.

At lunchtime on the third day, Ms. Drölma came home from work, beaming. "Yangdzom, you are a picture of health! Starting today you may wash the dishes, do the cooking, and all the rest." In the days that followed, she instructed Yangdzom on how to make the rice and the vegetables and supervised her as she took charge of preparing the meals.

Though Yangdzom wasn't a rich girl, she'd grown up in a humble household with two loving parents who took care of her, and she had no experience whatsoever of cooking. Moreover, all people in the country ever did was boil noodles and fry up some potatoes or radishes. At first, she was on the receiving end of several tongue lashings from Ms. Drölma due to her clumsiness and the poor taste of the food. But with a bit of time and practice, she got the hang of it. Now she knew how to cook things she'd never seen or even heard of before and had mastered a variety of dishes both hot and cold that were, as Ms. Drölma had first put it, a delight to see, smell, and taste. When mother and daughter got home, they were now greeted by a delicious feast. But this time of day—when the two of them came home to eat—was one of the most uncomfortable for Yangdzom, because Tenzin Lhadzé would wolf down her food, drop her bowl with a clatter, and leave the table without a word to anyone. Ms. Drölma ate slowly and barely touched her food, which forced Yangdzom to pretend that she was full long before she really was. It was just as Nyendrak had said: no one was going to make sure she ate, like they did in the country. Nor was it like at home, where you could just eat some porridge whenever you were hungry. Before long, Tenzin Lhadzé picked up on her discomfort.

"Yangdzom, you're not like me," she told her, "I can snack whenever I like. You only get three meals a day, so you should eat your fill." Lhadzé spooned some more vegetables into Yangdzom's bowl.

Ms. Drölma was not pleased. "This child! It's not like I locked up all the food and snacks in the house. If Yangdzom wants to eat, she can eat. Getting yourself all worried over nothing, like a rabbit worrying if the sky will fall." Before she'd finished speaking, Lhadzé banged her bowl down on the table, giving her mother a look of contempt as she stormed out, swinging her backpack over her shoulder. The sound of Tenzin Lhadzé slamming the front door made Ms. Drölma jump. She placed her bowl on the table and looked at Yangdzom darkly. "Are you satisfied? What a troublemaker you are. I've lost my appetite. You eat." She left the kitchen and went to her room to watch television.

Was this all my fault? Yangdzom wondered. Ms. Drölma was right, she thought—no one was controlling how much she ate; when she cooked, there was nothing wrong with making as much as she needed. There was nothing wrong with it at all, but still, this was a problem she had never had to consider before. She felt that if she did, it would be improper and disrespectful to the mistress.

She couldn't work out the reason for the rift between Ms. Drölma and her daughter, but their quarrels continued regardless. The sound of slamming was commonplace, and cracks began to develop in the kitchen and front doors. Now the main door, which was made of metal, was crooked and wouldn't close properly. When Yangdzom had first arrived at the mistress' house, she had been struck by the fact that that sturdy front door was damaged and had assumed that it must have been a burglar's handiwork. Now she knew it was because it hadn't been able to withstand the mistress' assaults.

When the fights died down, victory always belonged to Tenzin Lhadzé. That night, Lhadzé came home, went straight to her room, and closed her door firmly. Ms. Drölma sent Yangdzom to call her down for dinner. Yangdzom knocked softly.

"Tenzin Lhadzé, your mother wants you to come down for dinner…" she began timidly, but before she'd finished, Lhadzé issued an irate response through the door.

"God, you're so annoying! You two can just eat if you want to eat. Tell my mum I don't want to see her face."

Yangdzom could do nothing but go back downstairs, shaking her head. She had heard Lhadzé perfectly well, but she knew that relaying her message to the mistress word-for-word was bound to make her angry.

"Miss, Tenzin Lhadzé said that she doesn't feel like eating tonight," she told her.

Ms. Drölma's face clouded over. "That girl. All she does is antagonize me," she grumbled as she went upstairs to take Lhadzé a cup of tea. But Lhadzé's door remained closed.

"Could you please leave me alone. I have to study." Her daughter's refusal to come down for dinner caused Ms. Drölma to lose her appetite. Picking up her handbag, she headed out the door.

Tenzin Lhadzé's mood lifted the moment she was sure her mother had gone. She came charging downstairs and straight into the kitchen as though she had suddenly sprouted wings. She lifted the lid of the pan and looked inside.

"Yangdzom," she said, sniffing the leftovers, "can you heat up some food for me? I'm starving. I was so mad this morning I left without getting any money from Mum. I haven't eaten anything all day, and then she was in a mood with me tonight… anyway, Mum and I are always fighting. You should get used to it." As she spoke, Lhadzé frantically lit the stove and began to stir the vegetables with a ladle, giving the impression that she really was on the verge of starvation.

Yangdzom laughed. "You silly thing. What are you mad at her for? At the end of the day, she's your mother. You should be glad you have her—I don't have anyone I can call Mum. At any rate, no matter how angry you are, you shouldn't let your stomach suffer for it."

"My mum isn't like other people's. Anyway, I just don't like her. What's the point in talking about it? Can we just get the food made?"

Yangdzom heated up the dinner in a flash and set it down in front of her. Tenzin Lhadzé devoured a whole plate of rice and vegetables in an instant, as though she hadn't touched food in three days. That was the most Yangdzom had seen her eat since she'd arrived, and the most she'd seen her enjoy it. Only when Lhadzé had polished off her whole plate did she pay attention to Yangdzom again.

"Yangdzom, my mother has a bad temper, plus she's annoying. She's always picking on me. What I really can't stand is when she goes through my bag. Everyone's entitled to their secrets, and I've got things I don't want other people finding out about—especially my mother. I can't really say why I don't trust her, but I don't—not for a second. And without trust, how can you depend on someone? That's why I keep my door locked and won't let her in. You, on the other hand, seem like an honest person, so I'm going to leave you a key to my room. You can clean it once a week, but don't touch my stuff." Her speech concluded, she handed Yangdzom a single key.

Since she had come to the house, Yangdzom had always seen Lhadzé as an obstinate and disrespectful girl, but now that Lhadzé had confided in her, Yangdzom's viewpoint suddenly changed, and now she felt like a kind of older sister to her. Yangdzom untied the string of keys around her neck and added the key that Lhadzé had given her. "I never knew you had so many troubles. Don't you worry, I'll do as you say. But she's still your mother, so you should try to be patient with her," she said, smiling gently.

Tenzin Lhadzé shrugged. "It goes both ways. You can't clap with one hand."

"The two of you are like that folk song—'When the willow on that mountain bends, the poplar on this mountain bends; when they bend, they bend together, when they don't, it's each to their own.' But you're mother and daughter, so you shouldn't be so stubborn." Yangdzom was giving out advice now, settling into her role as older sister.

"I'll try my best. To be honest, I feel bad about it every time I argue with her. But you'll soon see what my mother is like. 'As the water gets clear, the fish appear.' Let's just drop it now. I have to go out this afternoon." She went to the bathroom to wash and get ready, later remerging with a small handbag over her shoulder. "Bye Yangdzom, I'm going to the movies with some classmates. Don't wait for me for dinner. Mum probably won't be home for dinner either, so eat whatever you like!" And with that, she took off like a bird in flight.

It was Sunday, so after Lhadzé and the mistress had both gone, Yangdzom was once again left alone in the house with Cub. It was the hot summer season. Lhasans love their leisure as much as they hate the heat, and they are loath to let the sun's rays touch their faces. This was because the fashionably inclined were concerned about their skin getting dark, and so they sported big tea-coloured sunglasses, sheltered beneath umbrellas, and wore slender gloves to prevent the sun from touching any part of their skin. At noon, when the sun's rays were at their hottest, few went out unless they had to, and the streets were tranquil. During those peaceful hours, Yangdzom could clearly hear the bees buzzing around the roses in the yard. Covering her head with a damp towel, she went to sit outside, but after being alone with her thoughts for a while she decided to go find something to do. At that moment, Tenzin Lhadzé's request popped into her head, and she went upstairs to clean her room.

She opened the door carefully. Inside, there was a large bed with a soft-looking mattress, on top of which her bedding lay in a messy heap. Her curtains were drawn shut so the room was dim, and there was a sour smell in the air. When she opened the curtains and saw the room clearly for the first time, she was bowled over. There was a TV, a laptop, and posters haphazardly plastered all over the clean, white walls: young, blonde-haired foreigners in nothing but their underwear, their arms covered in strange tattoos.

The blonde-haired foreigners weren't a pleasant sight at all, completely naked apart from their bras and little cloths like blindfolds covering their backsides. Even though she was by herself, Yangdzom flushed when she first saw them, and her heart started racing. After a glance, she didn't dare to look anymore, and she turned away to avoid them, busying herself by folding the clothes tossed on the bed and the chair. Once she had tidied the room, she locked the door again and went back downstairs. Yangdzom went to the yard and tried to focus her attention on washing clothes, but all she could think about was the bizarre figures she had seen on the wall upstairs. It was as though they were still watching her, or beckoning her—slowly, she found herself ascending the stairs again. She opened the door. She made a show of covering her face with her hands, but the gaps between her fingers grew larger, and she peeked through them to her heart's content. When she went back downstairs and looked in the mirror, she saw that her face had turned red as an apple. Feeling ashamed of herself, she swore that she wouldn't look at them again. After she had washed and dried the clothes, she placed them on the edge of Lhadzé's bed. She decided she should fix up the bed as well, and as she was doing so, she thought to herself how strange it was that city people weren't in the habit of making their beds. Ms. Drölma had also instructed her not to touch the bedclothes when she was cleaning her room. Her bed was much neater than Tenzin Lhadzé's, but Yangdzom had never seen it made—was it just so she didn't have to unmake it at night? She thought about how in the countryside it was considered taboo not to make your bed every day, and her amazement only grew. Now that she'd tidied Tenzin Lhadzé's room and washed all her clothes, Yangdzom went back to the yard to relax. She tried as hard as she could to suppress it, but the images on the wall appeared even more clearly before her, and she felt like today she had done something truly shameful. *How could I have looked at such things? From now on, I'll clean the room with my eyes half closed, and I won't look at those pictures!*

As time goes by and the world changes, so do people's habits and ways of thinking. It was in this way that her vows gradually fell apart and began to be ground down under the cartwheels of time. Now, whenever she had a free moment, those boys and girls on the wall winked and beckoned her seductively, and she began to clean the room even more often than Lhadzé had instructed. Cleaning the room in her spare time became an addiction. No one else ever came into the little room and it was now as spotless as a shrine. It became Yangdzom's pre-cleaning ritual to lie on Lhadzé's soft bed, enjoying her fill of the pictures on the wall.

Nyendrak didn't come home often, and Ms. Drölma had now entrusted all the household affairs to Yangdzom. The mistress enjoyed her mahjong and sometimes she wouldn't come home for lunch. At weekends, she was nowhere to be seen. On Saturday mornings, Tenzin Lhadzé would leave the house with a change of clothes in her backpack—school let out on Saturday afternoons, at which point she stuffed her uniform into her bag and put on her own clothes, did her hair up, and went out with her school friends, not returning until late at night. It was a Saturday just like this, and Yangdzom was once again alone in the hushed house with just the little dog, Cub, for company. Yangdzom didn't mind it when she had housework to distract herself with, but as soon as she'd finished her chores, her mind began to wander, and she could think of nothing but the pictures on the wall of Lhadzé's room. She missed her parents and she began to cry. She lifted Cub onto her lap and stroked his head as she poured out her troubles to him. "You're a prisoner, cooped up in here with nowhere to go, and I'm an orphan, all alone in the world. What a sad pair we make." Cub whined as though he'd understood, then licked her hand and nipped playfully at her fingers. It wasn't enough to lift Yangdzom out of her bleak mood—what she needed was her parents' love and the comfort of someone dear; Cub wasn't going to open his mouth and say anything to console her. Amidst her brooding, she recalled what Nyendrak had said before he left for the county: "My dear, this is your home. Don't be shy about eating your fill. No one here's going to encourage you to eat, like they do in the country."

She put Cub down gently and spoke her thoughts aloud. "That's right. Lhadzé and Ms. Drölma are out, and if I don't eat my fill then it's my loss." Entering the kitchen, she rummaged about for something to eat, but couldn't find anything that appealed to her. She grabbed a plate, stood there for a minute, then put it back. Cub, as though he could read her thoughts, fixed his watery eyes on her and wagged his tail, as if to say, *Can I have something?* She had nowhere else now—this was her home. She didn't have to worry about food anymore, yet that feeling of hunger that had plagued her when she first arrived had faded, and now, just like people in the city, her appetite had shrunk. In the end, she tore up a piece of dried meat and soaked it in a hot cup of tea for Cub. For herself, she dipped a dried hunk of steamed bread in the leftover tea and called it dinner.

Another sleepy Sunday morning, Yangdzom was relaxing at home when Ms. Drölma suddenly stormed in, screaming and shouting like an irascible vixen. "All the money's gone from my purse! Which one of you two had their filthy paws in my purse?" Yangdzom, thinking she was talking to Lhadzé, didn't say anything and continued to do her chores. Lhadzé had her headphones in listening to music and sat there as though all this had nothing to do with her whatsoever, thus Ms. Drölma's shouts went unanswered. The mistress stamped her feet in a rage, and her increasingly furious shouting boomed through the entire house. Now Yangdzom felt suddenly afraid, and she trembled, not knowing what to do. Tenzin Lhadzé, unable to take it anymore, ripped her headphones out and threw them on the floor, glaring at her mother furiously.

"Didn't I tell you, Yangdzom? The wind won't leave the prayer flags alone. Mum, screaming and shouting like this, don't you care what the neighbours will think? It's just a bit of damn money, what are you getting so worked up about? You blow thousands at a time on mahjong, don't you? But just to be clear, I have no idea where your stupid money is." When she'd said her piece, Lhadzé marched off to her room and turned on the TV, while Yangdzom went into the kitchen and busied herself with some chores, trying to escape the awkwardness of the situation.

'The wrath is aimed at the cow, but the calf takes the beating'— just as the saying goes, the mistress took out her anger on Yangdzom alone. She came at her with a face like thunder, spittle flying from her mouth. "If you didn't take it then who did? A ghost? Where's my money? If you're stealing money now, it won't be long before you turn the whole house upside down and cart everything off!" This latest round of abuse caused Lhadzé to re-emerge from her room in irritation. "I've only got one day off and you won't let me spend it in peace. And can you stop going round accusing people? I guarantee you blew it at the mahjong parlour. Ever since Dad went to the county you've done nothing but play mahjong. You don't care at all about me or my schoolwork." Lhadzé's outburst was like cold water poured on the bonfire of Ms. Drölma's wrath, and the mistress immediately fell quiet.

Ordinarily Ms. Drölma was a fearless woman, but before her daughter she was always stopped in her tracks, like a leopard encountering a lion. After a moment, Ms. Drölma picked up her handbag and left, muttering curses under her breath. Lhadzé approached Yangdzom. "I know my mum accused you unfairly. Don't let it get to you. She's got a nasty temper, but she's not a bad person deep down. I'm going to a classmate's birthday party today, so don't bother making lunch, just get some noodles from the place next door." She placed a five yuan note in Yangdzom's palm and headed out.

Despite Lhadzé's consolation, the weight of the accusation made Yangdzom unable to hold back the tears. Being called a thief hurt her deeply, and for the first time she felt that she wanted to be far away from this family. She stuffed her few toiletries and clothes into a plastic bag, but she hesitated on the verge of leaving: *Lhasa is so big, but where would I go? Where would I go?* She couldn't answer this question, so she took her things back out of the bag, sobbing, then went to the sink to wash her puffy face.

Where could she go? On her second day in Lhasa Ms. Drölma had taken her to the hospital, and she'd been to the nearby market a few times to get vegetables, but apart from that she hadn't been anywhere else. Nor did she have any relatives in the city. After she'd washed her face, Yangdzom lay on her bed in the kitchen, and as she stared at the gleaming ceiling, a voice came into her head: "Yangdzom, when you finish your errands, you should practice your reading and writing. And don't let what you already know slip. Having an education will make it easier for you to get a job later on." This was the second piece of advice Nyendrak had given her before leaving for the county. With these words ringing in her ears, it didn't feel right to just lie there, so she dug out a months old newspaper to practice her Chinese. As she studied the characters, she thought about how long it had been since she'd done the same for Tibetan, her mother tongue, and she wondered if she'd forgotten how to read and write it entirely. She shuddered, unable to read anymore.

2

YANGDZOM'S PARENTS WERE SALT-OF-THE-EARTH FARMERS. Farming families tend to have a lot of children, but they only had Yangdzom. Her father, Tenzin, lost his parents when he was young. Since he had no siblings and few other relatives to speak of, he really was cast out alone into the world. When her mother, Dekyi, entered into a relationship with her father, Dekyi's parents fiercely opposed it. But the pair had become inseparable and the outcome was inevitable—"if tsampa is mixed with water, it's certain you'll have to drink it," as the saying goes. The two young lovers were completely of one mind, and they defied Dekyi's parents and left to establish their own home. They were a clever and well-matched couple, and through their hard work they created a happy life for themselves.

One year, when the season for it arrived, they decided that Tenzin should go to Nagchu to pick caterpillar fungus. Dekyi prepared her husband some provisions for the journey—the best meat, butter, and tsampa they had in the house—and along with some of the other young folk from the village, Tenzin set off to Biru County in Nagchu to work the caterpillar fungus harvest. While he was gone, Dekyi woke early and slept late, taking care of all the responsibilities both on the farm and at home. Back then Yangdzom was a child blessed with a happy home. She was an exceptionally bright girl, and since her grades were better than any of her classmates', she was full of hope that the next year she would be going to the middle school in the county.

That year their livestock grew plump and their sheep multiplied. The cow gave birth to a healthy calf, as did their dzo. Tenzin returned with a bulging wallet from all the caterpillar fungus he'd sold in Nagchu, and like this their humble family became the envy of everyone in the little valley. Tenzin and Dekyi were the very model of a successful young couple, and the three of them together enjoyed the bliss of a happy family life. Flashing a bright smile, Dekyi told her husband about what had happened at home while he was away, and they discussed the family's future. Yangdzom, throwing her arms around her father's neck, tussled his mop of hair and wrinkled her nose.

"Dad, your hair smells! It needs a wash." Tugging on his ear, she pulled him over to the well. Her mother thought this was hilarious.

"What a little terror you are! If your dad washes his hair with cold water he'll catch a cold." She brought over a kettle of hot water, and Yangdzom applied a handful of laundry detergent to her dad's hair and massaged it in. Her mother pulled aside the collar of his shirt with one hand, and with the other gently poured warm water over her husband's head. Tenzin, feeling fully content with life, couldn't help but utter that proverb: "Happiness means home, love means family."

"Spring is half cold half warm, life is half suffering half joy"—another proverb, one as true as the words of the Buddha. They had been most blessed and fortunate that year, and they were full of hope that the following year would be even better. Tenzin and Dekyi discussed various plans for the coming months, and first of all they agreed to buy a TV before Losar, the Tibetan New Year. The county had issued twenty-inch colour TVs to a few families from the area, but after just a few months the colours had faded and eventually merged into one. At the same time, the sound became crackly, and if you watched it for any length of time, the TV simply refused to make any sound at all. If you gave it a bash out of exasperation, it made a sudden loud noise as though it could no longer take the pain, causing anyone in the vicinity to jump. "Hand-me-downs are never precious, donations are never valuable," some of the more garrulous villagers said, and it seemed they were right. So the family decided that before Losar, Tenzin should go to Lhasa to buy their TV, along with some other supplies.

On the day that Tenzin was to set out, Dekyi was bringing him some *chang* when the bowl suddenly slipped out of her hands and landed face down on the floor. The bowl, which had been passed down in the family from generation to generation, was their most cherished possession. The rim and the base were made of silver so it hadn't smashed to pieces, but there was now a big crack running through it. Dekyi shook her head, an anxious expression on her face. This was a not a good omen.

"Dear, I had a bad dream last night, and now this. I have a bad feeling. I think it's best if you don't go to Lhasa just now. There are lots of little shops around the village so we can get what we need for Losar here. Why don't we get the TV next year instead…"

Tenzin stopped her before she'd finished. He put his arm around her waist and caressed his daughter's cheek. "Don't be so silly. It's not the first time I've been on a trip. I'm always going away somewhere and it's always fine, so what's the harm in going to Lhasa? Plus I'll have the protection of the merciful Jowo Rinpoché, so nothing bad's going to happen. When I get back, the three of us can all watch the New Year Special together!" He left breezily, not even looking back, and went to catch the bus to Lhasa.

Tenzin had promised his wife that he'd be home in three days, which would be on the 25th day of the 12th month of the Tibetan calendar. Everyone in the village was busily preparing for Losar, and those who'd been away from home gradually returned one after the other. The 25th came and went, then the 26th and the 27th, and by the 28th there was still no sign of Tenzin. It was an old tradition that travelers should be home to celebrate New Year by the 28th. If you were still on the road come the 29th, it was considered inauspicious.

On the day of the 28th, everyone was excitedly bustling around preparing for Losar. Everyone except for Dekyi and Yangdzom, that is, who were waiting anxiously, all manner of thoughts running through their minds, completely incapable of getting ready for the festivities. They couldn't get their worries out of their minds, to the point where they could barely think straight.

Unable to sit at home and fret anymore, Dekyi took her daughter down to the crossroads near the village where all the returning travellers passed through. She stopped everyone she came across: "Have you seen my husband, my Tenzin?", but the only answers they got from the travellers were negative, each "No, sorry" causing her unbearable pain, like a razor blade slicing her heart. She began to tremble, the little flame of hope in her heart doused by cold water. As she clutched her mother's hand, Yangdzom felt cold inside, churning waters troubling her mind. She wanted to cry out as loud as she could, unable to repress her feelings any longer. Every shake of the head from the returning passengers brought the thread of their hopes closer to snapping, but still they remained, looking desperately into the distance.

Where could he go? He didn't have any friends or relatives in Lhasa. When they'd just got married, Tenzin had taken Dekyi to visit the city. The City of the Gods is vast, and there was no one they knew there. After spending hours roaming the city's streets and alleys looking for a suitable place to stay, they'd found a squalid, rundown guesthouse in a narrow alleyway that charged five yuan a night per person. There were six beds to a room, and nothing but the beds—you had to squeeze around them just to get in. On each bed there was nothing but a dilapidated mattress and a filthy duvet so faded it was impossible to tell its original colour. Dekyi liked to drink tea back home, but not only was there no tea there, the owner charged one yuan just for boiled water. To a cash-strapped country person, this was an outrageous fee, so during the day they did their best to get their food and drink at the market. At night, however, they still had to go back and sleep at the poky hotel, where it seemed hard to even breathe in the cramped room—in fact, apart from one tiny window, there was nowhere else that air could even get in. For Tenzin and Dekyi, who were used to the fresh country air, this was an unbearable torment. Lying awake in bed, they each had a vivid picture in their minds of drifting peacefully off to sleep on their porch back home, gazing up at the stars in the clear night sky.

They rose early in the morning and went to worship at the monasteries around Lhasa, and in the afternoon, they went to the Barkhor and the Tromsikhang market. In truth they were merely window shopping since they didn't have any money to spare.

Many people from the country liked to go around the markets even though they had no money in their pockets. But for Tenzin and Dekyi, no matter how much there was to see, aimlessly wandering around the shops did nothing but make them tired and hungry. After three circuits of the Barkhor, Dekyi was parched and starving.

"Tenzin, let's go back home," she said to her husband. "At least there you can have something simple to drink when you're thirsty and eat some porridge when you're hungry. All you get in Lhasa is a dry mouth and an empty stomach. You even have to pay money to go to the toilet. Jowo Rinpoché aside, Lhasa is hardly the realm of the gods it's cracked up to be. There's no place like home—no matter how humble it is. Let's go back."

His wife's words made Tenzin feel a pang of guilt—he felt ashamed that he hadn't given her a better life. Turning to his wife, he made an ardent vow: "Dekyi, you defied your parents and ran off to live with a poor orphan. I promise you I'll make lots of money from now on, and you'll be able to live just like those city women, wearing make-up and high heels and colourful blouses and eating nothing but the finest foods!"

This vow made little impression on Dekyi, who thought he was simply indulging in fantasies, draping himself in the rainbow. "Tenzin," she said, "those things have nothing to do with us, so quit daydreaming. So long as you keep loving me like you do now, I'll be completely content. How does that folk song go? 'We're fated to be a pair of swans; if all we've got to eat is reeds, at least we can eat them together.' If the two of us can live our lives together, that's all I could ever ask for."

Tenzin was so moved he had to hold back his tears. He wanted to take her in his arms and hold her tightly, but the Barkhor was so full of people he couldn't bring himself to do it. Instead, he squeezed her hand tightly and just looked at her lovingly, not uttering a word of what was in his heart. Dekyi noticed his unusual manner. "Don't get so attached to Lhasa, Tenzin," she said. "We still have our livestock and our fields to get back to." Tenzin decided not to correct his wife's misunderstanding. He silently vowed to himself that he would never let her suffer, and they returned home the next day as she wanted. When they got back, they threw themselves into the farm work with renewed dedication, and though they had no real money the earth was kind to them. They didn't have to worry about putting food on the table and clothes on their backs, and they lived an idyllic life.

3

THERE WAS STILL NO SIGN OF TENZIN, AND THE 30TH CAME around bringing no news at all. That morning, the village of Norling was filled with the smoky scent of singed hair as sheep's heads were roasted for Losar. Bad news reached Dekyi's ears that day, blown in on the same wind as the burning aroma. The news was brought by a young shopkeeper from the village named Dorjé. Tenzin had been hit by a car and killed in Lhasa a few days ago. "Good news stays at home; bad news travels far," as they say— before long, everyone in the little village had heard of Tenzin's fate. People wept and offered their condolences, and some shook their heads plaintively, saying, "No one will be celebrating Losar this year."

Normally, the hard-working villagers enjoyed themselves to the full during the once-a-year Losar festival. They gathered to eat crispy *khapsé* and drink delicious *chang*, and they celebrated with singing and dancing, welcoming in good fortune for the year to come. The morning of the 3rd was especially important; after setting out early to pray to the local deities and spirits, everyone got together to enjoy a song and a dance. But if someone in the village died, the festivities were abandoned and everyone turned to mourning.

Tenzin had been hit by a car on the busy streets of Lhasa on a thoroughly ordinary winter's day, and the heartless driver had fled the scene. Before the police got there, his body was just left in the street like trash. By the time the police did arrive there was no hope for him, and all they could do was take the body to the morgue. Since he didn't have any form of identification on him, the Metro Daily News on TV broadcast details of his physical appearance, what clothes he was wearing, and so on. Dorjé happened to catch one of these broadcasts, and as he listened to the description, he began to get the horrible feeling that they were talking about Tenzin. He remembered that a few days before Dekyi had been asking everyone who'd travelled to Lhasa if they'd seen her husband. The news report said the deceased was wearing a pair of long leather boots. When Tenzin and all the other young men went to pick caterpillar fungus, hadn't he bought a pair of boots like that in Nagchu on the way back? Dorjé went to the hospital to see if he could find out for certain whether it was Tenzin, all the while praying that it wasn't. But it was. He returned home without even concluding his business in Lhasa to deliver the bad news to Dekyi.

The news struck Dekyi like a bolt from the blue. She collapsed on the spot, and Yangdzom wet her pants in terror. The sleepy valley was rent with cries of anguish, and every man, woman, and child had tears in their eyes. Dekyi was brought back to consciousness by all the terrible commotion.

The next morning, hair unkempt and walking unsteadily, she set off for Lhasa, supported by Dorjé the shopkeeper. Except for the Chinese driver, a couple of Chinese passengers, and an old, white-capped Hui Muslim, there was no one else on the bus. Dekyi, Yangdzom, and Dorjé sat at the back. Mother and daughter hugged one another, and despite Dorjé's best efforts to console them, they sobbed for the entire journey.

Dorjé took them to the morgue at People's Hospital as soon as they arrived in Lhasa. Dekyi, not daring to go straight in, sat on the stone steps outside. After a while, Dekyi and Yangdzom followed Dorjé inside, keeping their eyes fixed on the floor in front of them. In a freezing room, a refrigerator drawer was opened and a cold, stiff body appeared before them. Even though he was barely recognizable, it took only a glance for Dekyi to be certain that it was her husband. With trembling hands, she touched his face and let out a heart-rending moan. Yangdzom knelt before her father's body, murmuring "Dad… Dad…" between her sobs. The tragedy of the scene even moved the two policemen standing guard to tears of sympathy for the mother and daughter's plight.

"He's already gone now. You shouldn't torment yourselves like this," said one of the policemen, trying to lift the mood and offer some comfort as they led mother and daughter away from the body.

"We're still working to track down the driver of the car. We don't have any leads yet, but I promise you we won't let him get away," said the other cop as he took two hundred-yuan notes from his wallet and placed them in Dekyi's hands. The older one likewise got two hundred from his wallet and gave it to Dekyi.

"In any case, you'll have to make arrangements for the deceased. Cremation is the cheapest and easiest option," he said.

As much as she was suffering, Dekyi knew that arranging her

husband's funeral was an important matter, so she pushed her pain way down, and with the help of Dorjé, took the money for the TV from her husband's body and made the necessary arrangements. For country people, it was hard to accept a cremation as a proper funeral, but in a big city like this where she didn't know a soul, she had no other choice but to shoulder that heavy burden.

Dekyi, tormented by the loss of her husband, went to the Jokhang Temple, to her only refuge: the statue of Jowo Rinpoché. She focused her complete attention on his loving countenance, clasping her hands to her heart in fervent prayer. "Blessed Jowo Rinpoché, I beg you, in your compassion and kindness guide my husband to the Pure Realm. And please, take pity on my poor unfortunate daughter."

Paying a visit to the Jokhang Temple after her husband's death, praying to Jowo Rinpoché, lighting butter lamps before him— these things gave her some small measure of comfort.

She returned home from Lhasa after offering her devotions, but her home was now bereft of its former happiness. The pain of her husband's departure and her longing for him kept her up at night and made her unable to eat during the day. She cried until her eyes were sunken and her face was gaunt, and before long, she joined her husband in death. The ill-fated Yangdzom was left alone in the world as an orphan. Dekyi's parents were still alive, but they were getting on in years, and their other relatives had many children of their own already. Yangdzom had no way to continue her schooling and had to go live temporarily with her grandparents. The villagers were concerned for Yangdzom's future, yet there was little more they could do but sigh in sympathy with her plight and donate some provisions—grain, cheese, bread. It was at this time that the village head recalled a recent meeting in the county where Nyendrak, the county head, had told him he was looking for a maid. Nyendrak was an official of no small standing, and moreover he was universally held to be a decent and trustworthy man. "If you can find me a good maid, I guarantee the girl will be well looked after"—this was his promise to the village head. After the village head talked it over with her grandparents, they decided that Yangdzom would be sent to work at Nyendrak's house in Lhasa.

4

IT WAS BUSINESS AS USUAL EVERY SINGLE DAY. YANGDZOM cleaned the house, washed the clothes, and prepared meals for the mistress and her daughter. She tried out new presentations of the dishes, new ways to cut the vegetables, and she changed up the hot and cold dishes, but apart from this everything was always the same, and even she was tired of the same old meals, let alone the people who were eating them. Yangdzom was now a woman of eighteen, and there was no holding back the radiance of her youth. She was tall and slender and her chest had unmistakably filled out. Even more striking than this was her eyes: almond-shaped, a sharp contrast of dark and light—it was almost as if they were speaking to you. A beautiful woman is traditionally called "doe-eyed," but looking at Yangdzom, it felt like such descriptions should be reserved for a select few women like her. That year, Nyendrak was reassigned from his county in the mountains to an office back in Lhasa, and his daughter, Tenzin Lhadzé, began the third year of high school.

Over time, Yangdzom had grown accustomed to the endless stream of curses and criticisms that Ms. Drölma directed her way.

With the return of Nyendrak, however, the mistress' mood became even fouler. She would fly into a rage over the smallest thing, ranting and raving at Yangdzom incessantly with accusatory undertones. But Yangdzom was a kind and forgiving person, and she thought to herself that it must be true what it says in the books about how a woman's mood will naturally sour when she reaches a certain stage in life, so it never occurred to Yangdzom that Ms. Drölma's anger was really directed at her.

Winter arrived even earlier than usual that year, as though it were trying to prove the validity of that old proverb: "Winter leaps out like an enemy; Spring goes unnoticed like a parent's love." Though the cold weather was upon them, Yangdzom's hands were still immersed in cold water as often as a duck's feet. Nyendrak, unable to bear seeing her work like that, went out and bought her a pair of rubber gloves from the market. This met with Ms. Drölma's disapproval. Her wrath provoked once again, she rounded on her husband with bulging eyes. "In the mornings you pour her tea, and at lunch and dinner you serve her food, and now as if that weren't enough, you're buying her rubber gloves! All maids wash the clothes and vegetables bare-handed, who uses gloves? How can she do the housework with rubber gloves on? I've never seen anything like it. If you're buying her gloves now, what are you going to get her next?" This was a different approach from her usual implicit accusations—now she was shoving and tugging at her husband, airing her thoughts in the open.

At work Nyendrak was a man with considerable status, but at home Ms. Drölma was boss. Normally he paid no attention to her tantrums, but this time he had reached the end of his tether. "You're always reading into things!" he retorted. "I just thought that Yangdzom was always slaving away at the housework, and sometimes she doesn't even have time for a cup of tea in the morning… unbelievable, absolutely unbelievable." He went upstairs and shut himself in his study.

"A happy home is scarce in samsara"—how true. Nyendrak and his wife both had good jobs and they were well off financially, but their clash of personalities meant that if they weren't fighting, then they were ignoring one another and sitting in complete silence. If your hearts aren't in harmony, no amount of wealth and possessions can make you happy. On top of that, Tenzin Lhadzé, who was more precious to them than anything in the world, was struggling at school and seemed to have no enthusiasm for anything. Her behaviour was a serious concern for the both of them.

Lhadzé was in the third year of high school now, but her attitude towards her studies showed no sign of changing, so her anxious parents decided to hire her a tutor. But Lhadzé, stubborn and contrary, responded in no uncertain terms: "If you've got so much money you want to just fritter it away, it makes no difference to me. Either way I don't want to study." Her parents were left with no choice but to back down. Though there were no changes in Lhadzé's approach to her schoolwork, there were big changes elsewhere: she dressed ever more ostentatiously, and she cut class ever more frequently. While other students were noisily making their way to school in the morning, Lhadzé rolled out of bed late, and by the time she did leave the house, she had her hair done up and was wearing makeup and stylish clothes, her school uniform stuffed in her bag. If she ran into a friend, she'd spend the whole day hanging around on the streets, and only if she couldn't find a partner in crime did she finally go to school. She would throw her uniform on just outside of the school gates, smooth down her hair, then go to class. Nothing the teacher said had the slightest impact on her behaviour, and what began as guidance soon turned into scolding.

She never came home on time, and on the rare occasions that she did, she never showed any intention of opening a textbook and studying. Instead, she spent all her time on her phone or looking in the mirror applying eyeliner and blush or combing her hair forward to cover her face, causing her naturally big, beautiful eyes to disappear behind an unkempt fringe. Sometimes, to get in her father's good books, she opened up a big textbook and pretended to study, lying on her bed and muttering to herself as though she were memorizing facts and figures. But all of this was for show: in reality, she was looking at her own face, reflected in a small mirror placed over the pages of the textbook.

One day Tenzin Lhadzé went into the bathroom and a long time passed without her re-emerging. Yangdzom happened to have an upset stomach, and she stood waiting at the bathroom door, hands clutched over her midriff. After waiting for an age, she was struck by a sudden pain, and she called out in agony.

"Achak Lhadzé, please hurry up, I can't wait anymore!"

"What's the matter with you?" said Lhadzé, flinging the door open irritably. "There's a toilet downstairs, what do you have to barge in here for?" Yangdzom didn't have time to answer, she simply pushed past her and went straight for the toilet. Lhadzé quickly shut the door, and after casting an irate glare at Yangdzom she brushed her teeth, washed her hands, and popped a piece of chewing gum in her mouth. Yangdzom had been too desperate to notice anything at first, but once her bowels were relieved, she finally realized that the room was filled with smoke. Lhadzé turned to face her.

"Yangdzom, don't say anything to my dad," she said, then left the bathroom.

Yangdzom was astonished. She pictured Nyendrak sitting alone and silent in his study; she saw his wrinkled face, his unkempt and greying hair. Nyendrak had moved back to the city now, but his refusal to pay any attention to his clothes or his appearance in general made him seem old and worn out. He had been reunited with his family, but no joy showed on his face.

Yes, he kept his troubles to himself and didn't say a word to anyone else. Perhaps that was the unique mentality of a man.

Right now, his biggest worry was his daughter. When he saw the way that she had become, he felt that he had failed her, and he began to show great concern for her education.

At the parent-teacher meeting at the end of semester, the young teacher proffered her opinions on Lhadzé's situation. She announced that Lhadzé's poor performance at school and her deteriorating conduct were not the sole responsibility of the school, but were directly connected to her situation at home. Nyendrak, sitting among the ranks of parents, bowed his head, his face burning with shame, completely incapable of coming up with a response.

He knew that what the teacher said was right, and he tried many times to discipline his daughter, but it was never any use. After he got home, he thought about the problem long and hard. He considered himself a reasonable and persuasive person, and felt that he was especially good at managing his subordinates, so why couldn't he manage his own daughter? He eventually decided that another sit down was necessary, a face-to-face discussion about improving her behaviour and her schoolwork. This plan received the backing of his wife, so one Saturday lunchtime, they all sat down and he strove to impress upon her the importance of education.

Lhadzé listened with her held tilted to one side, feigning agreement: "Yes father, I understand. I'll do as you say from now on." Her mother clearly wanted to interject at this point, but Lhadzé beat her to it. "I know what Dad says is true, but Mum, don't you start. I've heard it a million times. You're always at the mahjong parlour, you can't help yourself. And if not that, then you're always having a go at Dad. I think it's best if neither of us says anything about the other, it's always six of one and half a dozen of the other with us. I'm not an idiot, I know what I'm talking about." After a breathless pause, Lhadzé's anger suddenly increased, and she continued, now even louder and fiercer than before: "To be honest, if the two of you are really as worried about me as you say, then Dad—you wouldn't have left me here and gone to work in the country for all these years, and Mum—you wouldn't spend every waking hour playing mahjong. At any rate, the two of you aren't like other parents. Just look at yourselves—Dad is a capable and respected man, but as soon as he gets home, you're always putting him down. You both get in constant rows over the tiniest thing and won't give me a moment's peace. But let me get to the point: I hate you both." With that, she left.

This was a crucial time, just three months before the university entrance exams. But after this episode, Lhadzé left home and didn't come back, and they didn't hear a word from her. Her parents searched every nook and cranny of Lhasa but couldn't find a trace of their daughter. Nyendrak was sure that she would soon reappear, so he went to the school to request a leave of absence on her behalf, telling them that Lhadzé was ill.

As a result of Lhadzé's disappearance, Yangdzom earned a brief reprieve from Ms. Drölma's wrath. This truce, however, lasted only two days; come the morning of the third, Ms. Drölma was rifling through her purse, stamping her feet and waving her hands.

"I didn't count wrong this time!" she yelled, "I had two thousand in here for certain, and now there's only fifty left. Lhadzé stormed out in a tantrum the day before yesterday, so she didn't have the chance to take it. That means the thief could be no one but you!" She rummaged through Yangdzom's pockets, but all she found was a tattered one yuan note and a few coins leftover from buying vegetables. Yangdzom was terrified and shook with fright.

"Miss, I didn't take the money, I swear I didn't," she said, on the verge of tears. But in Ms. Drölma's eyes, her trembling and her timid tone were the reaction of a thief who knew she'd been caught. Not only did she refuse to believe Yangdzom's protestations of innocence, she seemed to take them as proof of her guilt. Her haranguing continued, spittle flying from her mouth.

"Look at your face! A godless thief might not own up to her crimes, but it's obvious just from one look at you!" Ms. Drölma marched into the kitchen and ransacked Yangdzom's bedsheets and her pillow, but since she still couldn't find her money, she hurled the whole lot into the yard and continued to tear them apart—and still there was no money.

Nyendrak entered the kitchen at that moment and intervened. "Yangdzom isn't the wicked person you make her out to be, Drölma. isn't it possible that you just misplaced the money?"

This just worked up Ms. Drölma into an even greater fury, and before he'd finished, she began roaring, "What girl? She's a sly fox, a vixen! Not only does she steal my money, she starts tearing up like she's been framed! She's stealing money now, and she'll be stealing your heart next." Still not satisfied, she was saying whatever came to mind now, continuing to point the finger at Yangdzom.

Yangdzom felt that since she hadn't stolen a penny, she had nothing to feel guilty or ashamed about, but with Ms. Drölma unleashing endless insults upon her, and with the mistress and Nyendrak now getting in a furious row, Yangdzom's fear grew and she couldn't help but burst into tears and tremble even more violently. A full-blown domestic dispute had broken out in the little kitchen, and it was only when she registered Yangdzom's terrified expression that Ms. Drölma paused her quarrelling, seemingly feeling a little uneasy. Nyendrak felt awful for the poor girl and wanted to offer her some comfort, but he didn't dare say anything in front of his furious wife. Usually, he accepted defeat and put up with it, but that day Nyendrak seized his wife's hand and pulled her into the other room, where their argument continued to rise in intensity as they traded accusations of blame for Tenzin Lhadzé's disappearance. Now they were going at it tooth and nail and there was no one to intervene. As though the time had finally come to get all the ill-will that had built up over the years out in the open, they poured out all their grievances at once, holding nothing back. After a while, the argument died down—whether because they had tired themselves out or because they had determined the victor was unclear. The courtyard was empty and no lights were on, making the house feel eerily quiet. Yangdzom didn't make dinner that night. In fact, she didn't dare touch a single thing in that house anymore.

Dusk fell slowly. Yangdzom lay on her bed feeling miserable, still crying. A short time later, Nyendrak emerged from the room. He came to the kitchen and tried to open the door, but Yangdzom had bolted it from the inside, so he went and spoke through the window instead, attempting to offer some words of comfort.

"Yangdzom, I know you didn't take the money. Don't be upset. You haven't even had dinner yet; if there's some bread left you should eat then get some sleep. It'll all be forgotten about in the morning." She didn't reply, but in her head, she thought, *How can it just be forgotten?* Yangdzom didn't get any sleep that night. She spent the whole time lying awake, crying and thinking about her future. Finally, she resolved to leave that house.

The next morning, she rose before dawn as usual and swept, cleaned, and made breakfast. It still wasn't light by the time she finished, so she collected Lhadzé's schoolbag from where she'd tossed it on the floor and looked for a pen and piece of paper. The backpack of a third-year high schooler ought to be full of books and supplies, but the only things she found in Lhadzé's that resembled a pen were an eyebrow pencil and some lipstick, and apart from the three unopened textbooks, there wasn't a single sheet of paper to be found.

She looked all over and couldn't find a pen anywhere. She took the eyebrow pencil and was about to start writing on the back page of one of the textbooks, but couldn't bring herself to do it. When she was at school she cherished her textbooks and never scribbled or doodled in them. At primary school, when the teacher was explaining the crux of the lesson, she would make careful note of the relevant passages, but she would never carelessly write in the textbook. These good habits had stuck with her. She put the book back in the bag, took a napkin from the table, and began to write:

Dear Mr. Nyendrak,

With the Buddha as my witness, I did not steal that money. I might be a poor orphan, but I would never stoop so low as to steal. If I ever did something so wicked, I would be insulting the memory of my parents. It pains me to see the two of you fighting because of me. If I stay here, there'll never be an end to it. For this reason, I have decided to leave. I don't know where I will go, but you don't need to look for me. I've taken an old bag with a change of clothes, some toiletries, and an empty chili paste jar as a cup. Apart from that, I haven't touched a thing in the house.

Yangdzom placed the note on the kitchen table, gently opened the front door, and left.

Her eyes were swollen from crying all night and she could barely see the road in front of her. She walked aimlessly for a while, never once looking back. It was still early and there was hardly anyone around, and the normally bustling streets felt quiet and still. Eventually, Yangdzom slowed her pace. *Where can I go? Where can I go?* She kept repeating the question in her head, but she had no answer. She could go back to Norling Village, but she had no family there anymore. Her elderly grandparents had passed away a few years ago, and now there was nothing left there for her. She continued to roam the streets with no destination in mind until suddenly she remembered Drölkar. A few days before, on the way back from grocery shopping, she'd run into her old primary school classmate on the street. When Drölkar was little she always had a runny nose, so all the kids called her Snotnose Drölkar. But now Drölkar looked every bit the white-collar urban worker: she wore smart clothes, carried a little handbag on her arm, and her hair was loose and unbraided, just like the fancy city women. From the look of it, she was doing very well for herself.

If Drölkar hadn't recognized Yangdzom in the crowd that day, Yangdzom would have paid no attention, thinking it was a Chinese woman who just happened to be calling out her name. Drölkar accosted her and gave her a breathless update: "Yangdzom, it's me—Snotnose Drölkar from Norling! I'm working at a Chinese company now, making several thousand a month!" Though Yangdzom was overjoyed to run into someone from home, she felt awkward about how long it'd been since they'd last seen each other. Instead of showing her happiness, she just listened to Drölkar with a deep sense of envy. Drölkar sized her up—her plain clothes, the two glossy black braids that had been plaited together and that hung down her back—and laughed. Fingering Yangdzom's plaits, she smiled. "It's rare to see traditional braids in the city these days. Seeing yours makes me think of home, of when we were little and we'd go off to school with our backpacks and hair all in plaits." Drölkar fell silent for a moment, then broke out in a smile again. "But that's all in the past. We're in the city now, and we're city girls. All the country kids are piling into the city these days, aren't they, as if they can get something without having to work for it." Drölkar's expression betrayed the haughtiness of someone who had long since become an urbanite.

In the face of Drölkar's stream of chatter Yangdzom was like a mute. She nodded along to everything Drölkar said, not knowing how to respond—the motormouthed Drölkar didn't give her the chance to, anyway. Before they parted ways, Drölkar took a pen from her handbag and wrote her phone number on Yangdzom's hand while she spoke. "Give me a ring me if you ever need anything!" As Drölkar walked away, Yangdzom waved meekly, still speechless. Her bright, almond-shaped eyes followed Drölkar's departing figure enviously. When she got home, Yangdzom copied the number onto a piece of paper and placed it securely under her mattress. Before she'd left the house that morning she'd retrieved the piece of paper and stuffed it in her pocket, and now, in her moment of desperation, those words came back to her: "Give me a ring me if you ever need anything!" She went to a public payphone at a roadside newsstand, took the number from her pocket, and was about to call when it occurred to her that she had to pay. She rummaged in her pocket again; all she had was one yuan and seven mao, but it was just enough for one phone call. Carefully, she dialled the number Drölkar had given her. It rang several times, but no one answered. She called twice more, and the second time, a drowsy voice answered in Chinese: *Wei?*

By now Yangdzom had learned to read a bit of Chinese and she could stumble her way through a conversation. "*Zhuoga zai ma*" she said into the phone tonelessly. Drölkar could tell that her caller was Tibetan, and she switched languages. "What is it? This is Drölkar," she snapped irritably. Without waiting for a response, she continued her sleepy grumbling: "What the fuck, I'm trying to sleep here."

"It's Yangdzom, from the same village as…"

"Right, yeah. I just got off work. If it's nothing important call me after lunch," she said sluggishly. The moment she heard the familiar accent of home, Yangdzom couldn't help but burst into tears, and between her sobs she blurted out everything that had happened.

Drölkar snapped to as if she'd had a basin of cold water poured over her head. "What the fuck!" she yelled into the phone, "The bastards, how could they! Where are you now?" Yangdzom, however, couldn't even guess where she was, let alone give the name of it. She asked the owner of the kiosk what the place was called. The woman eyed Yangdzom up and down before she answered; Yangdzom's lips were as dry as sandpaper and her eyes were so swollen they'd almost closed up.

"We're close to Lhalu Bridge, so that's what everyone calls the area," she said eventually.

"I'm at a payphone kiosk near Lhalu Br–"

Before Yangdzom could finish relaying her message, Drölkar cut in: "Got it. Wait there. I'm coming with my little puppy dog to get you."

Yangdzom waited for Drölkar, wondering why she needed to

bring her dog with her. Soon a black car pulled up next to her and a pretty Chinese woman with big sunglasses leaned her head out of the window and shouted, "Yangdzom, Yangdzom!"

Just how many Yangdzoms are there in Lhasa? she thought to herself. She glanced in the direction of the car, decided it had nothing to do with her, then went back to staring into the distance. The pretty woman got out of the car.

"What's the matter with you! It's me, Drölkar. I'm here now so you've got nothing to worry about. Show me the way, let's go find them. You ran around waiting on them hand and foot for five whole years, and now you've got nothing to show for it but an empty bag and the clothes on your back. Even if we forget about the false accusations, they at least have to hand over your wages for all these years." Drölkar was panting with indignation.

"Achak, I don't want to go. Forget about the money. I can't bear to face all her abuse and scorn again. Best to keep my head down and live peacefully. Besides, when I stepped out of that door this morning, I swore to myself I'd never go back through it." No matter how much Drölkar insisted, it was no use, and she was forced to give in.

"Well I suppose you're right," Drölkar said as she wiped away Yangdzom's tears. "What was the point in staying with those bastards anyway, they don't even see us countryfolk as human beings. Those sons of bitches will get what's coming to them." Drölkar broke into a smile, then turned and nodded her head towards the young man sitting in the car. "What do you think? My little plaything. What can I say, I'm just too gorgeous for my own good. They all flock to me like flies on meat."

Yangdzom gave her a shove. "He'll hear you! What puppy dog— it's a boy."

Drölkar laughed heartily. "You! In the city these days, if you've got a mistress who's younger than you, she's a 'little bee,' and if it's your boytoy who's younger than you, then he's your 'puppy dog.' It's just what people say now."

Yangdzom didn't feel like any of this had much to do with her. "Achak you're such a funny one," she whispered. "Here I am down on my luck and you're kidding around."

Drölkar placed her hand on her heart. "Don't you worry, girl. You've got your sister here now, your Achak." She opened the back door of the car and ushered Yangdzom inside. Drölkar got in the passenger side next to the young man, did some brief introductions, then they set off for her apartment, Drölkar and her 'puppy dog' laughing and chatting all the way.

5

THE CAR STOPPED AT THE ENTRANCE TO A LITTLE ALLEYWAY. Drölkar got out, quickly pressed two fingers to her lips, and waved. "*Bye!*" she said in English. The boy returned her gesture. "*Bye!*" he said, then drove off.

The alley was extremely narrow and packed on either side with little shops. With the exception of a few Chinese clothes shops, the vast majority of them were general stores run by Chinese Muslims. The shelves out front were piled high with clothes: *pangdens*, shirts, *chubas*. There were also people from the country selling local produce and farmers from outside the city selling yoghurt, milk, vegetables, and the like. Since they didn't have their own stalls, they leaned against the walls and spread out their wares in front of them, making the alleyway even narrower than it already was, leaving just enough space for a person to pass through, but certainly not enough to ride a bike. The most striking stalls among them were the ones with little shelves full of CDs of popular music. One place was playing songs by the Khampa singer Yardong from a loudspeaker, one was playing Nangma Toeshey, one was playing Indian music, and one was playing Teresa Teng songs. It felt more like they were having a singing contest than competing for sales.

The second and third stories above the shops were all apartments. Those with money bought a house on the outskirts of the city, rented out the apartments they owned here, and led a pleasant life. Those without money gathered all their family into one room of the apartment and rented out the others to supplement their income. It was fair to say that this was the best resource available to them.

At night, the entire street was just as noisy and active as it was during the day. This area used to be called Dargyé Gardens, but the only remaining evidence of this was a solitary metal sign hanging at the end of the street, blue and rusted, on which you could just barely make out those words—words that no one actually paid attention to anymore. The people who lived there now came from all over the place, and while no one knows who exactly replaced "Dargyé Gardens" with the new name of "Liberty Gardens," most people now referred to it as the latter, and very few were aware of the former.

Drölkar and two of her friends shared a small rented room on the second floor. It seemed that they all had the same kind of job, as they went to work around nine in the evening and came back at dawn. The other residents around the courtyard didn't normally pay much attention to the people who came and went, but since the three girls were different, they secretly referred to them as the "night owls." No one knew what they did for work, and no one asked.

The rent was two hundred a month, not including water and electricity. In this city, there was no better or more fitting home for them. The courtyard around Drölkar's apartment was a large square, and it contained people of all different ethnicities who spoke all different languages, but they all had one thing in common: each of them had plastic or clay pots of varying sizes outside their windows or by their doors, filled with all manner of Himalayan flowers: Drölmas, Kelzangs, Hetas, Tratiks. Spring, summer, autumn, and winter, sparkling, dewy flowers of every colour bloomed in the pots. This was a good habit that had been passed on by the old inhabitants of the place, and it turned the otherwise chaotic courtyard into a beautiful paradise.

Drölkar opened the door to her apartment and waved Yangdzom inside. "Girls, I'm exhausted, I didn't get a wink of sleep this morning," she said, tossing her handbag onto the bed, where she also had Yangdzom take a seat.

The room was extremely cramped, as though it were trying to rival the narrow alley outside. There were three beds pushed up against the walls and an old table in the middle of the room, on top of which was a small thermos for tea. Behind the door were three neatly arranged washbasins, each of which contained its owner's toiletries. That accounted for all the furniture, and if the three women did own anything else, there wouldn't have been anywhere to put it. Drölkar's two roommates were each fast asleep on their beds and didn't seem to notice their presence. Looking around the little room brought to mind the one place Yangdzom didn't want to think about: the big house. Why does there have to be such a vast gulf between people, she wondered? She started to feel anxious about her own future living situation. Making a conscious effort to suppress the thought, she continued to examine the room. What stood out most was the large mirror on the back of the door. Whenever one of the girls came in, the first thing they would do was look in this mirror; when they were going out, they crowded around it, fixing their hair and makeup, and only left when they were satisfied. Yangdzom also noticed the overpowering scent of perfume that pervaded the tiny room, stinging her nose.

Yangdzom scrunched up her face and was on the verge of saying something to Drölkar when something struck her, and she stared at her surroundings once again in mute silence. The scene before her eyes was so at odds with Drölkar's appearance and her clothes, and Yangdzom couldn't get her head round it. Drölkar seemed to know what she was thinking.

"You're surprised, huh? The tsampa gets tastier as the day goes on. There's better things ahead of us, you'll see." Drölkar fell silent for a moment, then lit a cigarette and slowly exhaled a cloud of smoke. "You worked all that time at that official's house, slaving away like Isaura from that TV show, and all you got to show for it was an accusation of theft. You're better off staying with us, at least you'll be free. Most of the people round the courtyard don't know what we do and they're not nosy like country folk. Everyone minds their own business and keeps to themselves here. That's the thing about city people, they're open-minded. There's room for everyone—good, bad, rich, poor. You don't need to ask me what I do. It's a job people don't like to talk about anyway, so it's best if you don't know. You can squeeze in my bed with me for now, and we'll figure out what to do later all in good time." As

Yangdzom listened she watched the practiced manner in which Drölkar smoked and studied her face with increasing confusion. Yangdzom suddenly got up off the bed, her expression one of amazement. *Is this woman in front of me really Achak Drölkar, my old school friend, the one I've known all my life?*

Yangdzom's strange reaction made Drölkar uncomfortable. Looking back into Yangdzom's apprehensive face, she said, "Don't be so shocked! My bed's clean, at least." Drölkar put her hand on Yangdzom's shoulder and made her sit back down. She gently took the bag that Yangdzom was clutching in her hands and opened it; it contained nothing but some old clothes, a few toiletries, and an empty jar. Drölkar laughed. "Look at this! Is this your pay for all these years? This skin cream costs two yuan a bottle, it's *Dabao*, the stuff people in the country use. Starting tomorrow, this is your hand cream. You're in the prime of your life, if you use this crap on your face, you're throwing your youth away. Look, you can use mine. These are all from South Korea and they cost me a fortune. Your face is your own, but it's others that have to look at it all day. Girls these days put skincare number one, more important than food." She took Yangdzom's towel and comb and put them in her own washbasin. "I haven't had breakfast yet either," she went on, "let's go get something to eat. In the afternoon we'll go shopping and get you a handbag and a new outfit."

Yangdzom couldn't get those words out of her head: "It's a job people don't like to talk about anyway." *What is it that Achak Drölkar actually does? Please don't let it be that bad thing people talk about!* Still not daring to ask her, she trotted after Drölkar like an obedient child. They passed through the narrow courtyard and into the bustling street.

Drölkar took her phone from her bag and spoke in Chinese

to someone named Sun, who she asked to come and meet them for tea. A short time later a bald Chinese man showed up at the teahouse. He was an ugly, hairless little man with bloodshot eyes, but his wealth was nevertheless apparent from his expensive designer clothes and the thick gold chain around his neck.

He sat down and said to Drölkar, "Is the sun rising in the west today? Every time I ask you out you put me off with some excuse."

"I'm in a good mood today," said Drölkar, flashing an artificial smile.

He declined to respond to this, and turned instead to Yangdzom. "Is this little lady a new arrival at the Rose?" he said, flashing an artificial smile of his own. Drölkar gave him a fierce slap on his bald head.

"Pervert! She's my little sister, come from home to see me. Don't you dare lay a finger on her."

"Whatever you say, baby." He rubbed his head, then turned to Yangdzom and nodded slightly by way of introduction.

The three of them ate breakfast then sat for a while drinking tea, after which, at Drölkar's request, they went to the mall. As Drölkar picked out a new outfit and a handbag for Yangdzom, she said to her, "Just you watch, I'm gonna take a hatchet to that dirty old bastard's wallet today." Yangdzom looked at one of the price tags and couldn't believe her eyes—maybe they'd added an extra zero by mistake? She looked again and confirmed the amount in horror: it was more than three hundred yuan.

"Achak, let's go to the Tromsikhang instead. I've got a change of clothes anyway, there's no need to take advantage of people." She went to put the clothes back, but Drölkar retrieved them.

"I didn't even pick the expensive ones. Just look at him! He calls me his mistress. Says if I give him a son he'll buy me a house in

Lhasa. But let's leave that for later." Yangdzom was troubled by this, but she didn't say anything.

After taking a thousand-odd yuan from old baldy's wallet, Drölkar said to him, "I've put you out today. Next time I'm free, I'll show you a good time." Yangdzom felt like she was holding her hand out begging, or like she'd just robbed someone, and her heart pumped and her face turned red. In her mind she thanked the man standing in front of her over and again, but not a single word of gratitude came out of her mouth as she hid herself behind Drölkar's back. Drölkar, registering her discomfort, turned to the man with that artificial smile again. "The two of us have something we need to take care of today, so we'd best be making a move. We'll go for tea another day."

After they went their separate ways, Yangdzom heaved a deep sigh. "Achak, I've never been so ashamed in all my life. A complete stranger just spent a stack of money on clothes for me, and I don't feel good about it at all. You should wear these yourself, Achak. I wouldn't dare wear such nice things. It's my karma to be a servant, so what's the point in getting dressed up all posh?"

"You're too meek, that's why people push you around," Drölkar said. "You served those people for five years and in the end you left sobbing, wiping away your tears, nothing but an empty sack to your name. We have to look after ourselves in the city. We have to be smart, and not let ourselves get hurt…" Drölkar continued to offer her advice as she led Yangdzom to a restaurant on the main street, where they had a quick bite to eat. By the time they got home it was almost seven, and Drölkar's two roommates had already gone out. Drölkar changed her clothes and did her makeup, painted her lips bright red, and insisted that Yangdzom wear the new outfit they'd bought that day. The clothes make the woman—when Yangdzom put on her new outfit she looked like a completely different person. But Drölkar still wasn't satisfied, as Yangdzom's face remained plain. When Drölkar tried to apply some powder to her cheeks, Yangdzom jerked her head away.

"Achak, I don't want that stuff on my face. When we were redecorating Mr. Nyendrak's house last year we put paste like this on the walls then whitewashed it, and we had to do a good few coats. This'll be no different!"

Drölkar laughed. "That's certainly one way to put it. But our work is at night, and there's a reason city folk call us 'night owls.' People who are in the know call us 'cats.' But cats or owls, we all look like tigers and leopards when we're under the streetlights. We put paste on our faces and cat skin on our bodies."

That night, Drölkar took Yangdzom to the Rose, a bustling, glittering nightclub in the city centre. This was where Drölkar worked. It was the kind of place that was packed at night and empty by morning, and it was full of Tibetan hostesses like Drölkar, but equally full of young, attractive, prettily dressed Chinese girls. They entered through a door emblazoned with lights into a large, multi-storied building filled with little glass-walled rooms; the floor under their feet was also made of glass, and beneath it were twinkling, multi-coloured lights and a variety of plastic flowers. To Yangdzom, who had spent all of her time cooped up in the mistress' house, this was an incredible sight, and she was virtually stopped in her tracks. Fearing that the glass floor beneath her might give way, she treaded softly as she followed Drölkar through the club.

Drölkar, clearly well-acquainted with the place, navigated them to a large, smoke-filled room, which contained several heavily made-up, red-lipped Chinese girls whose clothes showed off every aspect of their young bodies—thighs, arms, shoulders—and there was also a Tibetan woman, puffing away on a cigarette as she watched TV. When the two of them entered, every pair of eyes in the room immediately fell on Yangdzom.

"Girls," Drölkar began in Chinese, "this is my little sister. She's just come in from the country to look for work. Since I'm the only family she has in the city, she's staying at my place for now until she finds a job." They all seemed relatively indifferent to this, with the exception of the Tibetan girl, who inspected Yangdzom closely then gestured for her to come sit next to her.

"You don't need to go looking for a job, sweetie, you can be a hostess here with us. It's pretty easy work, and you can pull in a good wage without much effort." Yangdzom thought about what Drölkar had said and the way she made herself up, and she finally understood everything. She rose in a flash and made to leave, but Drölkar headed her off.

"Where are you going? There's nothing at my place but a cold empty room. Don't worry, I won't drag you down with me. But do you think that we do this work 'cause we like it? I've done every job out there in the last few years—I waitressed in a restaurant, worked in a shop, filled up cars at the petrol station—but the pitiful wages are barely enough to support yourself. It's not enough to pay for my dad's medicine, never mind sending money for my brother's schooling. Where else could I go to get all the money for that?" When she'd finished, she was breathing heavily and tears were rolling down her cheeks. The others were watching Drölkar now, their eyes welling up. The Tibetan girl handed her a tissue.

"Don't cry. How can you get by in the city without money in your pocket? The customers will be arriving soon, why don't you go fix your makeup."

Yangdzom realized now that these women all harboured deep troubles, a sharp contrast to their dazzling, carefree surfaces. They hid the pain they felt inside under a mask of smiles. People scorn and despise their profession, but they don't know how hard things are for them. Yangdzom was overcome by a sudden feeling of compassion. A moment later a young Chinese man wearing a white shirt, a black waistcoat, and a red tie entered the room and called the women's names one by one. "Magnolia" he called first, and the Tibetan girl left the room indifferently. Next, several of the Chinese girls exited the room as the man reeled off the names of more flowers. When he called "Dahlia," Drölkar turned to Yangdzom. "You wait for me here and watch TV. We'll go home together when my shift is done," she said, then left the room. So Yangdzom sat by herself, watching TV and waiting for Drölkar. By one AM there was still no sign of her. Shortly after, amid a chaotic mix of sounds—the television, the music outside, the drunken shouting, the horse-hoof clacking of high heels coming and going—she was lulled into a fitful sleep. She was awoken by the chill of the early hours, but still Drölkar hadn't returned, so she curled up on the couch and kept watching TV while she waited. Drölkar finally reappeared just before dawn. She brought with her a nauseating mixture of odours—cigarette smoke, alcohol, perfume—and Yangdzom felt like she might actually be sick. Drölkar was drunk and was in no state to leave immediately. Only after she had rested on the couch for a little while did the two of them leave the Rose.

They walked for a while under the sparkling streetlights until they came to a restaurant—seemingly one of Drölkar's regular haunts—where they grabbed a bowl of noodles, then they got in a taxi and headed home. This was Drölkar's daily routine, and it was clearly all second nature to her. When they got back to the room, the owners of the other two beds had already returned, but they were deep asleep and didn't stir. Drölkar wiped off her makeup with a tissue, pulled off her clothes, and fell into a blissful sleep the moment her head hit the pillow. Yangdzom was wide awake, like an animal on the prowl, replaying the tumultuous events of that dreamlike day in her head.

She lay in the narrow bed, not daring to turn over, waiting for it to get light. When it did, she wanted to get up as usual, but she couldn't bring herself to. *What would I even do if I got up?* She thought. The other girls had been up all night and she didn't want to disturb them, so she just lay there.

When the other girls awoke just before noon, Yangdzom, too, got up and sat on the edge of Drölkar's bed. Now, finally, she got a good look at the other two. The first thing the girls did was rush off to the public toilet, and when they came back, all of them washed their faces and started putting on their makeup. Drölkar pointed to the one looking in the mirror—it was the Tibetan girl from the night before.

"This is Achak Dzomkyi. At the Rose she goes by Magnolia. She's the queen of the club." Pointing to the Chinese girl who was washing her face, she said, "This is Xiao Li. At the Rose they call her Cassia. She's the baby. No one there calls me Drölkar—I'm Dahlia."

"She was scared to death when she saw our shady mugs last night—half goddess, half demoness!" said Magnolia mischievously.

Yangdzom turned to Dahlia. "Achak, I'm not a good talker, there's no way I could do the job that you do. I don't want to, either. I'm good at manual labour and housework. Please, will you help me find something?" She bowed her head slowly and stood there rubbing her palm.

"Sweetie, I once had an easy life, living like a princess," said Magnolia, gently stroking her hair. "But even princesses have their ups and downs, and now here I am, having to work as a lowly hostess. But this job isn't so bad. Lots of people struggle just to make ends meet, and here you get to eat delicious food and wear nice clothes. Some people might even envy us." She sighed, as though she'd only just thought of something. "I'm going to say this from the heart. You are a pure white snow lotus; we're all sewer flowers. If we can help you find a good job that suits you, what could be better than that." Magnolia's speech, well intentioned as it was, seemed to be full of contradictions.

Yangdzom didn't pay much attention to any of this, as though she simply didn't want to hear it. In fact, she wanted to get out of the room as fast as she could. "I'm planning on staying here until I find a job. I can't remember the names of all these flowers, and I'd feel strange calling you that. From now on I'll just call everyone 'Achak.'"

On a morning when white clouds soared and danced in the pure blue sky, Yangdzom and Dahlia hit all the restaurants and shops on the main street looking for work, but everything they found that day either satisfied Yangdzom but not Dahlia, or it satisfied Dahlia but not Yangdzom. They ran around until their legs were sore. In the afternoon, they finally found her a dishwashing job at a big teahouse, where they agreed on a five hundred yuan monthly salary with free meals included.

Now that Yangdzom had a job, she left early in the morning and came back late in the evening, so she barely saw the others. When Dahlia got home around dawn Yangdzom was fast asleep and snoring, her shoes soaking wet, and the hands sticking out from under the duvet were bleeding and covered with chilblains. Dahlia couldn't bear to see this and she resolved to find Yangdzom a better, less punishing job. One morning, Dahlia got up earlier than normal and went to take a look at the place where Yangdzom worked.

It was a snowy, freezing cold winter's day. Yangdzom was wearing a large plastic apron. Cold water was pouring from the tap in front of her, under which she was washing a mountain of dishes as she sang a little tune to herself. It was the dead of winter and Yangdzom's shoes were soaking in a puddle of cold water beneath her feet, and her hands, covered in blisters, were immersed in the cold water with the dishes, like swimming ducks.

Dahlia stomped across the water-logged floor without a thought for her shiny high-heeled leather shoes. She seized Yangdzom's hand and pulled her away, unfastened her big plastic apron, and tossed it to one side. "You are not spending one more day here!" she thundered, panting with anger. She tugged at Yangdzom's hand, trying to take her away, but Yangdzom was bewildered.

"Achak, what are you doing? Who told you to come here?" In a muddle, she went to pick up the apron, but Dahlia snatched it from her and threw it back on the floor. At this point, the woman in charge came over.

"What is all this? People are trying to work here…" Before she'd finished, Dahlia cut her off, still breathless with rage.

"She's my little sister. You can forget about her wages. I'm taking her."

"Ha! You think she can just come and go as she pleases?" said the manager, clearly unwilling to let Yangdzom leave.

"OK, so where's the contract then? Let's see it!" This was a bit of legal savvy she'd picked up from the owner of the Rose; it was also the first bit of wisdom this city had taught her. She hadn't known a thing about the law when the Rose was hiring, and she'd signed the contract after the briefest of glances. Now, that contract had become like an invisible, inescapable chain wrapped around Dahlia's body.

The manager couldn't hide her disappointment. "Where am I going to find another girl as hard working as this?" She took five hundred yuan from a little cash box and placed it in Yangdzom's hands. "My dear, you only worked here twenty-five days, but I want to pay you for the full month. If you don't find a better job later on, you're welcome back here anytime."

Yangdzom, helpless and forlorn, looked from the manager to Dahlia. "I'm not leaving, Achak. I'm happy here–"

"You might be happy now, but when you're lying in bed, your hands and feet all shrivelled up, five hundred yuan won't even be enough to pay for your medicine, and it'll be too late for regrets by then. Just look at your hands—they're completely covered in blisters. Lady, the least you can do is spend one or two yuan on a pair of rubber gloves for your dishwashers." She grabbed Yangdzom's hand and pulled her away again. Yangdzom turned back and bowed to the boss, her way of showing her gratitude for the full month's wages. But Dahlia's words had plunged the manager into deep thought. Her face turned red from shame and she couldn't utter a word as she watched Yangdzom leave, her eyes filled with remorse.

6

From then on, Dahlia made Yangdzom stay in her room during the day, and at night the two of them continued to squeeze onto the same bed. For the time being, she wouldn't let Yangdzom go look for work, either. But Yangdzom couldn't put up with this state of affairs.

"Achak, I can't just go on like this, no job, no food. I need to find work."

"Just leave it for now. Stay in the room and rest up. Even if you don't find a job, I can look after you." She tried to press several hundred-yuan bills into Yangdzom's hand, but she pushed them away.

"I'm just one mouth to feed, I've got no family to support or anything. But you, Achak…" Yangdzom trailed off.

"Yangdzom, no matter what, as long your Achak has a scrap of food to eat, then you'll never go hungry."

The two women decided that, from then on, all of their joys and sorrows would be shared. Nevertheless, there's always a big difference between ideas and reality, and there was no way Yangdzom could just shut herself up in the empty room all day as Dahlia wished, so one morning Yangdzom crept out while Dahlia was still sleeping to resume her job hunt. Though she did this for several days in a row, she still couldn't find anything suitable.

Yangdzom returned to the room with heavy steps, her shoulders slumped in defeat. Flopping down on the bed and listening to the jumbled-up sounds of the music coming from the alley had now become her daily routine. Every time a new song came out, the pirated discs were never far behind, and everyone—the disc hawkers, the teahouses, the general stores—began blasting it at full volume, as though they were competing to see who had the loudest speakers. In this way, she soon absorbed the lyrics and melodies of all the new tunes, just by lying there.

There was now only four hundred yuan left of the wages that Yangdzom's boss had given her. While out roaming the streets over the last few days, she'd spent a hundred yuan on sweet tea and noodles just to keep herself going. She took the remaining four hundred from her pocket, and as she looked at the notes in her hand, she wondered what she could do with it. Set up a little stall? It was nowhere near enough. How long would four hundred last? She should stop going out, to save money. That day she waited for Dahlia to get up, which she eventually did around noon, her hair all in a mess. Dahlia looked at her with concern.

"There's nothing for you to do here, Yangdzom, so why don't you sleep in a bit?"

"Achak, I've been cooped up in this room for a long time now. I feel like a pig just lying round here all day. How about you lend me some money, then I can set up a little stall on the night market."

"You don't even dare look people straight in the face, how are you going to sell things at the market?" Dahlia said, astonished. "You need to be sharp and ruthless to be a market trader, otherwise you'll get eaten alive." Yangdzom's slim hope burst like a bubble.

Now she left home in the morning and wandered the shops aimlessly, just like she had a few days before. Around noon she got a bowl of noodles on the main street. She wanted to get a cup of tea, too, but she didn't dare spend the change. When she'd finished the noodles, she had accomplished half her day's work. In the afternoon she wandered the main streets again, half-heartedly looking for work, and that was how she passed the day.

As the scarlet evening clouds fell into the west, people were busy rushing back home, but since Yangdzom didn't have a home of her own to return to, she decided to do three circuits of the Barkhor. At that hour, the Barkhor, the heart of the old city, was lit up brilliantly by the evening lights, making it especially beautiful. Gradually, more and more people appeared, leisurely circumambulating and chanting their *manis* under the pretty lights. Their presence irked Yangdzom. Abandoning the Barkhor, she slowly made her way back to the apartment. The girls had long since left for work, and their clothes were scattered haphazardly all over the tiny room, making the place feel even more cramped. Unable to put up with the mess, she tidied up the clothes and gave the room a good clean.

Perhaps this was a habit she had picked up from working at Nyendrak's house. Wherever she went, if she came across a mess she wanted to tidy it, and if something was dirty she wanted to clean it. Once the little room was spotless, she had nothing else to do, so she lay down on Dahlia's bed. Her stomach ached with hunger and growled non-stop.

Ever since leaving her job at the restaurant, she hadn't even managed to stave off the daily hunger, let alone eat a nutritious diet. That day she'd had nothing but breakfast and she felt weak— even when she was climbing the stairs to the apartment she felt like she could barely make it. The sound of blaring music and anarchic shouting rose up from the street, mixing with the growl of her stomach, and after a while she fell into a soft, hungry sleep from which she awoke almost immediately.

The aroma of the girls' instant noodles wafted into her nose, mingled with the scent of their perfumes. She wasn't normally a fan of instant noodles, but that smell aroused her appetite and her mouth watered, suddenly craving them. What a treat a bowl of noodles would be right now! Just then, the scent of the perfume, even more powerful than the noodles, overcame Yangdzom and the mismatch of smells managed to suppress her hunger for a moment. Her stomach gave another long rumble, then she passed back into unconsciousness.

In her dreams she was about to wolf down a steaming hot bowl of instant noodles. She opened her mouth as wide as a cave, but not a drop would go in, and she panicked. She awoke right then, her mouth still wide-open, deeply disappointed that she hadn't managed to eat that bowl of noodles.

7

ONE ORDINARY WEEKEND, YANGDZOM WAS COOPED UP IN THE room as usual, and once more she told Dahlia that she didn't want things to go on like this.

"I know it's hard to find a good job right now," Dahlia said. "You have to be patient, so let's just keep looking until the right one comes along. I know it's hard for you being stuck in the room all day. Why don't you come with me tonight? It'll take your mind off things at least. As long as you keep to yourself no one will bother you. Those dirty old men wouldn't dare lay their hands on a girl like you anyway. They're very clear on who they can and can't mess around with." She made Yangdzom put on the clothes the bald Chinese man had bought for her, then she took her to the Rose.

At the club, Dahlia was called into a small private room, where four men were waiting. She brought Yangdzom with her and made her sit off to the side. She first made an announcement for Yangdzom's benefit: "Gentlemen, this is my little sister. You may amuse yourselves with me as much as you like, but not with her. She's not cut from the same cloth as the rest of us."

Yangdzom was eighteen now, but she'd never been in close quarters with men like this before. She sat with her head bent, not daring to look at them, wiping her sticky palms on her trousers, her sweat-soaked shirt clinging to her back. Dahlia sat in the middle of the four men, smoking cigarettes and pouring their drinks. That's when they broke out the dirty talk. Yangdzom, even more embarrassed now, went to the bathroom to escape the discomfort and splashed her face with cold water. She looked in the mirror, took a deep breath, and feeling a little calmer now, went back in. Dahlia was nowhere to be seen, and nor was the hairy fat man.

"Have some beer, sweetheart. And pour some for us," said one of the men, inching closer. She retreated, stammering. The man's bloodshot eyes were fixed on her scornfully. "If you dare come to this type of joint, you're best off dropping this sweet and innocent routine. She said you're not cut from the same cloth, but who's gonna buy that when you're in a place like this?" He grabbed her and forced a drink into her mouth. Yangdzom was terrified and tears were running down her cheeks, but the three men pawed at her as though they were tanning leather and the smoke from their cigarettes filled her mouth. She did everything she could to defend herself, but she was like an ant under an elephant's foot. When she lost the strength to resist any longer, she sobbed as she murmured to herself, "The world is large, but there's no place for a girl like me; The City of the Gods is vast, but there's no home for a girl like me." Yangdzom had never touched alcohol in her life, and the sharp, bitter liquid revolted her. The three men, taking it in turns, kept pouring.

Before long, her head was spinning, her whole body was numb, and her mind was fuzzy. That was when one of the bulky men led her out of the club and to the nearby Union Hotel, where he took her into a room and pushed her down on the bed. This was where the clients of the Rose took the young women who sold their youth, and that night, the man treated Yangdzom just like one of those working girls. When he began tearing at her clothes like a hungry jackal, she had a moment of clarity. "No, stop," she cried, mustering all the strength she could to push him away and lurch off the bed, but the man grabbed her like an eagle seizing a lamb and tossed her back down, ripping off the new clothes the bald Chinese man had bought for her.

She knew exactly what was about to happen to her, and her heart started racing with dread. She tried to resist with all her might, but compared to that fearsome man she had all the strength of an eight-year-old child. She pushed and shoved, but in the end, she had lost the strength to repel him, and all she could do was plead with him again and again, "Please, let me go." *It's finished, everything's finished*, she thought, absolutely petrified. After a while she fell completely still, like a corpse. When he saw the blood on the sheets, he laughed with satisfaction and she cried in despair. He kissed her once on the forehead, tossed five hundred yuan onto the pillow, then left, giving her a parting pat on the ass.

Dahlia emerged from a room in the Union Hotel smoothing her hair and rushed back to the Rose to check on Yangdzom. She found no trace of her, nor of the other men. She knew immediately that something wasn't right. She went from room to room looking for Yangdzom, but she was nowhere to be found. She sensed then that something terrible had happened, and in the same instant she thought of the Union Hotel. Dahlia raced back to the hotel, retracing her route from a moment ago. She pounded on door after door in a frenzy, but most of them were locked and no one answered. Finally she came to a little room in a secluded corner of the hotel—the door was ajar. She went in and found Yangdzom lying on the bed, the covers still pulled down, naked apart from the shredded shirt covering her chest.

Her face was ashen. She wasn't moving and wasn't sobbing. An unbroken line of tears ran across her cheek and into her ear. The instant that Dahlia saw Yangdzom, she was brought back to that snowy winter night. The tragedy that had befallen her on that horrible night played in her mind like a movie. She knew exactly what had happened, and she wept with remorse and threw her arms around Yangdzom's neck. "It's all my fault, but I never thought anything like this could happen. The bastards, the absolute bastards… I hope they rot in hell…" She wailed in agony, but it was as if there was no connection at all between the Rose, the Union Hotel, and that terrible, heart-rending sound— the nearby nightclub was still bathed in glittering electric light, and the sound of the music suddenly seemed clearer. The hotel sat silently, enveloped in the darkness, as though nothing whatsoever had happened there.

Dahlia was tormented by guilt and felt an unbearable pain like her heart was about to split in two. Her body trembling and still rent with sobs, she removed her coat and covered Yangdzom. She tried to lift her up, wanting to get her out of that disgusting place as quickly as possible, but Yangdzom was stiff as a corpse and wouldn't move a muscle. She mustered all her strength to hoist Yangdzom's leaden body, and when she did, she saw the blood drops that stained the bedsheet. The scarlet blood was even redder than the lanterns that hung from the ceilings of the rooms in the

Union Hotel. At that moment, Yangdzom finally said something—but her first words weren't to do with how that inhuman man had forced himself on her.

"Oh my goodness," she said, "Achak, won't we get in trouble with the owner? I've made a mess of their sheets."

Dahlia stroked her hair. "How does a dummy like you still exist in the world? It's all my fault. I promised to take care of you, to protect you, but I failed. We're sisters, and from now on we share all our joys and sorrows."

"Don't be sad, Achak," said Yangdzom, her expression completely despondent. "This must be my bad karma. How does that old saying go? 'You can't avoid your karmic lot, just like you can't wipe the wrinkles off your forehead.'" Yangdzom gathered her concentration and dragged herself up off the bed and the two of them walked out of the hotel, Yangdzom leaning on Dahlia for support.

On the clean white bedsheets of the Union Hotel, the blood from Yangdzom's body and the scarlet hundred-yuan notes left by the fat man lay dried-up and wilting, as though in sympathy with Yangdzom's miserable fate.

Yangdzom lay in bed staring at the ceiling, not eating, not sleeping. Her mind convulsed like turbulent ocean waves and her insides felt like they were on fire. She remained that way for four days. The girls didn't know what to do and were worried sick. Dahlia, unable to take it anymore, took time off work to be with her. She knelt by the bed and told Yangdzom exactly what happened to her on that freezing, snowy winter night, leaving nothing out.

When Yangdzom heard Dahlia's terrible story, she finally began to cry. Her dry, cracked lips quivered, but not a word of comfort escaped from them. When the girls got up the next morning, however, Yangdzom, too, arose unsteadily. The girls were overjoyed to see her out of bed; Cassia fetched some water for her to clean up with, and Magnolia went to the alley to buy her some breakfast, still unwashed and in her slippers. Dahlia clutched Yangdzom's hand with tears in her eyes.

"It's so good to see you up. I would have died of shame if you kept staying in bed. There's no escaping the miseries and hardships life throws at us. We have to keep going, no matter what." One of Dahlia's tears fell onto Yangdzom's icy hand, its heat bringing a tiny bit of warmth to her cold heart. She squeezed Dahlia's hand.

"You mustn't blame yourself, Achak. It's my karma, there's no fighting it. If you could know your fate, you'd avoid your mistakes. No one could have known that such a terrible thing would happen, so don't be too hard on yourself. It's my bad karma. I'll never be chaste again after that day, but I'm still here, I still have to keep living, so what choice do I have? I failed to take care of the body my parents gave me, and I've been dead inside since that day. Now I have nothing left but my tarnished body. I'm going to come and work with all of you at the Rose. Achak, I'd like you to have a word with the boss for me. Once a white cloth gets stained, it can never be clean again."

Yangdzom went with them to the Rose from then on, deaf to Dahlia's protests. For the first month, she began by learning all the duties of a hostess: how to dance, hold her drink, make toasts, and smoke cigarettes. The hardest thing was learning to dance. The young Chinese dance instructor at the club taught her by grabbing her waist and showing her the moves. Since her young body, softer than butter, had been brutalized by a man whose name she didn't even know, the merest touch of a man's hands made her uneasy.

When he came close, she backed away; when he looked up, she looked down. She stared at her feet, completely incapable of focusing on the movements and the music.

If it had been any other girl, the dancing instructor would have lost his temper long ago. But he could tell that she was timid, reserved, and gentle, not sly and silver-tongued like the other girls at the club, and he kept his patience as he ran her through the one-two-threes. Yangdzom had never danced before. She'd only ever seen men and women dancing up close like that on TV, and if she wasn't treading on the instructor's feet, she was getting her feet caught under his. The other girls fell about laughing when they saw this.

"You can do it!" they yelled. "Yangdzom, you're pure and delicate, just like an azalea. That's your new name! You can do it, Azalea!"

When she heard this, her movements became even clumsier. The new name sounded strange to her, and she glanced at the dancing instructor, embarrassed. "I'm sorry, I really can't get the hang of this. Besides, can the clients even dance when they're drunk?"

The instructor gave her a disapproving look. "Let me tell you, even if they're blackout drunk, that has nothing to do with us. And whether they're able to dance, or even know how to dance… that has even less to do with us. Our job is to make sure we get our money before they pass out on the floor."

Before too long, not only had Yangdzom mastered the dancing, she had loosened up her stiff hips, too. Now her supple waist swayed as she served those dirty men, an artificial smile plastered over her natural expression, as though there was nothing to it. Moreover, she always made sure to get what was hers before they blacked out drunk. Unlike before, she no longer had to worry about where her meals would come from, and with the passage of time, she cried less, and thought about her parents less, too.

She became just like the other girls: doing her makeup, smoking cigarettes, drinking beer, raising toasts—all these things had become second nature to her. Now, customers grabbed her by the waist and kissed her on the lips, and she didn't feel embarrassed in the slightest. Nevertheless, she still couldn't stand the smell of perfume, cigarettes, and booze on her body, and even worse was the shit-eating breath of those vile men—it was insufferable torture every time she smelled it.

One major change from her previous circumstances was the wads of hundred-yuan bills that filled her purse—more than she'd ever even laid eyes on, let alone touched with her own two hands— as well as the designer clothes and gold jewellery she couldn't have even dreamed of before. She immediately struck anyone who saw her as beautiful and elegant.

One day, someone from the Red Cross was handing out fliers on AIDS prevention on the main street. They were giving out free condoms, so Cassia grabbed a handful and stuffed them in her bag. When she got to the club, she handed a few to Azalea. Azalea took the condoms in her hand and inspected them—they obviously weren't for eating, and they didn't look like they'd be much good as bags, either. She idly unwrapped one and put it over her finger.

"Hey, what is this, a finger glove?" she said, waving her hand back and forth.

The girls in the room laughed so hard they had to clutch their bellies.

Dahlia took her to one side for a serious word. "In this miserable line of work these things are an absolute necessity. It was stupid of me, I should have explained this to you before. From now on, whenever a client wants special services, you must use a condom."

Her face turned as red as an apple and she shoved the condoms into her purse without a word to Dahlia. Yes indeed, it's the way of the world that things go from being unknown to known, then from known to familiar, and finally they become second nature. Gradually, she learned all about these things, and she also learned how to use her natural good looks and newly-acquired feminine wiles to make those men get out their wallets and fork over the cash. The kind of embarrassment and shame she'd felt when Dahlia raided that bald Chinese man's wallet had now vanished like morning dew under the sun. She had come to understand the way things were: when those vile men, driven by lust, took almost every part of a woman's body for themselves, why should she care about taking a bit of their money? To put it candidly, the women there had no shame, and the men who went there had no conscience. A lot of their money was dirty, too, so there was even less reason to feel ashamed about taking it.

She spent her daylight hours like the other girls from the Rose, roaming round the shops whiling away her time, occasionally calling some of the big clients to come and hang out at the teahouse and maybe play a round of cards or mahjong. Magnolia was the oldest of the four of them, but she still frittered away her money as carelessly as a little girl with never a thought of saving a penny. Cassia was the opposite: she was frugal and planned carefully, treating money like it was her life and never spending recklessly. She didn't even have any toiletries of her own; she just scrounged off the others. She did, however, always take it upon herself to keep their room clean, and she even helped the others do their laundry. Ever since Azalea had joined their ranks, Cassia's voluntary duties had decreased. Azalea, humble by nature, cleaned the room of her own accord, so though the little room they occupied was cramped, it became spotlessly clean. Since Azalea was the youngest, the others all looked out for her, and in turn, Azalea came to see them as her own family. Unlike the other girls, Azalea was fond of reading magazines and newspapers, and the other girls got in the habit of picking up a book with a pretty cover for her any time they passed by one of the second-hand book stalls in the alleys.

They all had one thing in common, and that was that they never brought a man to the apartment and they never made a noise in the courtyard. They didn't make small talk with the neighbours— if they ran into them, they just gave a quick smile and a nod of the head. This was a policy Magnolia had laid down when they first arrived. As she said, "It's best if people don't know what we do. It's not exactly a reputable profession. They're ordinary people, and there's no way they'll ever show up where we work—they couldn't afford to, anyway." The neighbours referred to the four girls as the "night owls," but no one ever asked them what they did, which it seemed was their way of doing them a courtesy.

Azalea hadn't been at the Rose for long, but her monthly earnings were second only to Magnolia's, earning her the title "little princess." In fact, she had grown to be just like a real princess: her long legs, full breasts, supple waist, and alluring eyes made the lustful patrons of the club jump on her like a parched elephant seeing a lotus pond. Having undergone a baptism of fire, she was no longer the meek little girl she used to be. She met every client with a stony-faced expression, paying no attention to their age and looks, caring only for who arrived first and who flashed the most cash. In fact, she let the vile clients put their hands anywhere they liked, completely indifferent. When a client requested it, she went with him to the Union Hotel, and as long as he produced the money, she let him do whatever he wanted with her. When she gave her body to them, she felt nothing, not even the loathing she'd felt with that first man. She considered her job done the second they crawled off her, and she didn't hesitate to thrust out her delicate hand to collect her money, a plastic smile on her lips.

There was a brief time when a new customer started frequenting the Rose. He was a sixty-something year old Tibetan businessman, and unlike the usual degenerate clientele, this man came early in the evening and then left early too. After a few days spent getting the lay of the land, he took a special liking to Azalea and began showering her with tips and little gifts. After they had known each other for a while, he started buying her jewellery and calling her "my little treasure."

One day, the old man took Azalea's hand and said, "I'll give you five thousand yuan a month and get you an apartment. You'll be my mistress, and I can have you all to myself." At first, she wasn't too sure what a "mistress" was, but she thought that even though he was a bit long in the tooth, if she could get someone to give her a home and provide for her that wouldn't be bad at all, and so she accepted. In anticipation of the old man sweeping her away from the Rose any day now, she stopped giving special services to other clients, instead just providing the standard entertainment—dancing, toasting, and drinking with them.

When Dahlia and Magnolia found about this, they took it up with the old man.

"You don't need to give Azalea five thousand a month. Just get married, make it legal, and take her to live with you." When he heard this, the old man was astounded, and his narrow eyes widened.

"Well of course I'm fond of the young ladies—every man under the sun is. But to abandon my kids, my own flesh and blood, and my wife, who's been by my side for my whole life through thick and thin, and then run off with a prostitute? I'd need my head examined! A man like me, living openly with a woman of your kind—I'd be setting fire to my reputation."

After that, the old man stormed out of the club and never showed his face there again, and Azalea's dream of living a respectable life vanished like a rainbow. After this episode, she determined that this job was the best she could hope for, and she resolved to carry on, even clearer now in her mind that this was what her karma had allotted to her.

8

ONE TYPICALLY LIVELY NIGHT AT THE ROSE, A MAN STAGGERED in and demanded to be served by the most beautiful woman in the place. Magnolia was the queen of the club and Azalea was the little princess, but Magnolia was already off with another client, so the boss sent Azalea to serve him. Despite the man's drunken, boorish behaviour, he had about him an undefinably dignified, masculine air that set him apart from the usual clientele of the Rose. Most of the men who came to the Rose did the rounds of the other bars first before turning up roaring drunk, stumbling around and shouting, all while sporting their flashy, expensive clothes. This man was likewise wearing a handsome designer outfit and he carried a small leather attaché case under his arm. He ordered a luxurious private suite, and Azalea showed him inside. He sat on the sofa as though he were very familiar with the place and proceeded to carefully inspect Azalea's face, not uttering a word.

This type of client was common, too: they didn't jump on the girls right away like a wolf on a piece of meat, and they didn't request special services either; they groped, they kissed, they drank, and they left. For that reason, the girls were always glad of a client like that. With his type, you could take it easy, accompany him in drinking, and make two or three hundred yuan for one evening's work. It was easy money.

"What would you like to drink, brother?" said Azalea with a smile, dutifully and gently.

"Don't rush. Come and sit next to me," he said seriously. Taking Azalea's hand, he drew her towards him, then began stroking her back and nuzzling her cheek. He ordered ten cans of Lhasa Beer and had her pour for him. "What's the point in drinking alone?" he said as he drained his glass, "You have to drink with me."

Yangdzom had her wits about her, and sensing that something wasn't quite right, politely refused with the excuse that she couldn't hold her drink.

"Fine. If you won't drink it, I'll have to pour your beer somewhere else." He picked up another beer, emptied its foaming contents on her, then scrunched up the can and threw it at her. Azalea remained unmoved—he was just putting on a show, she thought. She took a handkerchief from her pocket and wiped the beer off her face.

"Brother, it looks like you can't hold your drink that well, either. Here, let me get you some water." She poured him a glass of water and turned on the stereo. Teresa Teng's "Drunken Tango" drifted from the speakers.

"Oh spare me!" he grunted irritably as he loosened his tie, and she swiftly shut the music off. He grabbed her hand and pulled her into his lap. "How about I take you to the Union Hotel? That's where you all go, isn't it?" He gaped at her body, his eyes bulging. There was something about the man's behaviour that wasn't quite the same as the usual lecherous men. All of a sudden, she remembered the girls describing a man just like this, a cop, in charge of the "clean up the streets" campaign the police had waged the previous winter. She was increasingly certain that he wasn't just killing time like the regular drunks. She decided to play dumb.

"Brother, are you talking about the water? That's free. You paid for the room, it's included."

"I'm talking about paying for you…" he said, getting impatient.

"Brother," she laughed, "don't kid around. I just dance with the customers and pour their drinks. I don't do anything indecent like that." This made him laugh sourly.

"Well then, are you included with the price of the room too?" He rose, smoothed down his hair, and walked out. There's a toilet in the back room, she thought—what's he going downstairs for? Just as she was puzzling over his strange behaviour, the lights in the club went out, the music shut off, and the whole place was filled with screams and shouts. A moment later the lights came back on, and the Rose fell silent. The revelry in the main hall had ceased, and clients and hostesses were pouring out of the private suites. Next door at the Union Hotel, men and women were likewise being marched out of the rooms.

Before long, everyone had been herded onto the dance floor. The normally cocky, overbearing men all looked like they'd been hit over the head with a rock: they stood quivering, looking at the floor with their necks wound in. The women were hugging one another, sobbing and shaking. Among them, the most humiliated of all was Magnolia. She had been dragged out of the Union Hotel wearing nothing but her bra and underwear. Azalea removed her shawl and threw it towards Magnolia, who was standing right in the middle of the main hall. "Here, cover yourself up, quickly," she hissed, but she was overheard by a young policeman, who picked up the shawl from where it had landed on the floor and tossed it back. One by one, Magnolia, all of the other women, and all the men were taken to a dimly lit corner where the police questioned them, being sure to record everything and take detailed notes. The men no longer spoke in the booming, self-important voices they used with the hostesses; now they squeaked like mice, so quietly that only the man taking notes could hear them. In the face of the policemen's imposing presence—the immaculate uniforms, the national crests glittering grandly on their caps—the clients lost their usual domineering swagger and became completely cowed, like a puppy who's fallen into a pot of stew.

Azalea was the last to be questioned. Like the other girls, tears of shame and dread had caused her makeup to run down both cheeks. "This way," said one of the cops, giving her a shove. Azalea wrapped her arms around one of the columns by the dancefloor, moaning, "I won't go, I won't go!" This made the cop angry. "Still talking back! Just look at yourself, a young girl like you, and what are you doing with your life? A pathetic, shameful thing like this." He shoved her harder, at which point the 'client' from earlier came over to intervene. "She just helps out here," he said, then went to retrieve the shawl from where it remained on the dancefloor and wrapped it around Magnolia. On that peaceful night, many of the girls—Magnolia and Dahlia among them—were taken away amid the wailing of the police sirens and the burning red of flashing lights. Azalea went after the police car, but it fled off on the road before her, leaving nothing but a cloud of dust in its wake.

She stumbled after the car for a few more steps, but she couldn't run in her high heels. She took them off and walked barefoot, carrying her shoes in her hand and crying. It was the middle of the night now, and apart from the odd car coming and going, the streets were deserted. She went back to the apartment in despair. Cassia was already home and asleep. When Azalea entered, Cassia shifted in her bed and turned to her, bleary-eyed. "What a disaster tonight was. Good thing I had no clients, otherwise I'd be done for," she mumbled with relief. Azalea, ignoring her, tossed her handbag onto the bed and went to look at herself in the mirror on the back of the door—her mascara ran down her cheeks in two big tracks, mixing with her blush to create a riot of colour. The woman in the mirror wasn't the famed beauty from the Rose—now she looked like a demoness. "Go to hell!" she screamed, slamming her first into the mirror. "What's the matter with you," said Cassia, "don't do that. This isn't the first time it's happened. They'll be home in a few days when the storm passes, and the Rose will be back to business as usual, you'll see. You should get a few thousand in cash ready though, I'm out of money." Her words came out lethargically, and when she was done, she turned over and fell straight back asleep, snoring away peacefully.

Azalea wasn't very happy about Cassia's indifferent attitude, but those words gave her small comfort: "this isn't the first time it's happened. They'll be home in a few days when the storm passes." She washed her face and took out the bank card for the account Dahlia had set up for her—there was over ten thousand yuan in there, which ought to be plenty. Feeling slightly more at ease, she went to bed.

A few days later she received a phone call from the police, telling her to come in and pay their fines—four thousand yuan per person. Elated, she went straight to the bank, withdrew all her savings, then went to pick up Dahlia and Magnolia. Her sisters were deeply moved that Azalea had come to their rescue when they needed it most. "Bastards," Magnolia said, "normally we'd get a heads-up well in advance. Maybe that stingy old boss at the Union skimped on his bribe. I need to get a bit of money saved up from now on—enough to pay the fines, at least."

Four

1

DAHLIA'S FAMILY WASN'T WEALTHY, BUT SHE HAD TWO loving parents and a clever little brother. Her father was a stonemason, well-known in their region, and thanks to his artistry, all their basic needs were provided for and both Dahlia and her little brother, Tsering, were able to attend school worry-free.

But Dahlia soon fell victim to that old saying: You can't avoid your karmic lot, just like you can't wipe the wrinkles off your forehead. When she was in the second year of high school, her father fell off the roof of the new house he was building for them. He didn't lose his life, but he broke his hip and was in hospital for six months. His body, once straight as an arrow, became crooked as a bow. By the time he got home from the hospital he wasn't in pain anymore, but his injuries were chronic and all he could manage to do was a few odd jobs around the house, meaning that all the back-breaking labour in the fields fell entirely to her mother. Dahlia was getting good grades at school, but due to her family circumstances, she had no choice but to give up the education she cherished and return home, her bedroll bundled on her back. She had another reason for coming home as well: to ensure that her brother, Tsering, could go to university. All her unrealized ambitions were now passed onto him. Tsering was a quiet and thoughtful boy, and he performed exceptionally well at school. He didn't let his sister down, coming first place in the county in the high school entrance exams, an achievement that earned him significant renown in their tiny corner of the world.

Despite the fact that Dahlia had traded her bookbag for a hoe and a shovel and swapped the brightly lit classroom for the wide-open fields, toiling on the land with her mother only made them enough to fill their bellies. They had no other sources of income, and without money, they had no way of paying for the medicine her father needed. On top of that, his accident meant that he wasn't able to put the roof on the house, and the unfinished structure stood in the middle of the village like a blackened camel's hump. The other villagers muttered to each other indistinctly every time they walked by it, and the thought of it made both mother and daughter restless and anxious. Faced with this terrible situation, her mum cried whenever she wasn't working. But Dahlia was young, she could read and write, she'd had some education, so she was sharper than her mother in that regard. She felt there was no way to improve things for her family if she stayed in the village, so she decided she had to go to the city. There, she could make some money to pay for the completion of the house, for her father's medicine, and, most of all, for her brother's schooling. When she told Tsering her plans, he looked into his dear sister's eyes and made a promise. "Achak, you've sacrificed so much for me and for this family. I won't let you down, I swear."

And so, like all the other villagers who had gone to the city to make money, Dahlia packed up her bedding, prepared some tsampa, and bade farewell to her home. She left with a smile on her face, her heart full of hope.

Like many other young women who'd made the move from the country to the city to find work, Dahlia started out washing dishes at a teahouse, where she earned three hundred yuan a month. She sent two hundred of that home, keeping a hundred for herself for rent and food. This was as frugal as she could be: several girls from her region all shared accommodation, and the cost of the rent, plus the water and electric bills, was fifty yuan each a month, leaving her with just fifty a month for food and other necessities.

The teahouse was always packed with customers, and Dahlia took the opportunity to ask around about getting a higher paid job, which is how she ended up working as a petrol station attendant. That job also took care of her electricity and water bills for her, so she stayed there right up until Tsering graduated from high school. Sometimes, when there weren't any cars to deal with, she would sit, happy and idle, reading a magazine or the newspaper. When Tsering finished high school, he was accepted into a university in Beijing. While the family was over the moon, they were also worried about the cost. Fortunately, he received a five-thousand-yuan scholarship from the university, and the County Bureau of Education chipped in with a stipend of three thousand yuan, which just about covered his travel and other expenses.

Dahlia's wages gradually rose to fifteen hundred yuan, so the four hundred a month that she initially sent to her brother also rose to five hundred a month. The money his sister sent was only enough to cover his food and nothing else, but never once did he trouble his family for more. Though he certainly could have qualified for full financial aid on the basis of his grades, his impeccable conduct, and his family situation, he never even considered applying for it. He remembered one New Year back home, when they'd seen all the various government departments and organizations giving aid and cash handouts to poor families on TV, even wrapping *khata* scarves round their necks, and they received it all bowing and scraping. Dahlia had said, "They're getting handouts and they're standing there wearing *khatas* like it's some glorious thing. That proverb says it best: 'Didn't give alms in my past life, now I'm poor in this one; now I'm poor, I can't give alms.' We have to rely on our own two hands to get by in life." That had always stuck with him, and he'd vowed to himself, like he was carving it in stone, that no matter how difficult things got he would never ask for financial help. He thought, too, of what his sister had wrote in one of her letters: "No matter how bad things get, you can never stop fighting." These words had increased his determination to be self-sufficient, and he'd even written them out neatly on a piece of paper and stuck it on his wall.

He treated the words on the wall as a guiding light for his studies and for his life as a whole. They gave him great encouragement. In his second year of university, he got a job delivering newspapers in his spare time, which earned him two hundred yuan of pocket money a month. He was still poor, but he was happy.

All of his dormmates had pictures of NBA or football stars plastered on their walls, but the only thing on his was the piece of paper with that phrase on it. Everyone asked if they were the "wise words of one of your Tibetan lamas," and he just said "yes," offering no further explanation. After that, no one asked about the piece of paper anymore.

At the petrol station, Dahlia was always counting off the days until the end of the month, thinking of payday, always yearning for it to come faster. She'd been asking some of the customers she knew if they could help her find a better paid job, but she had had no luck. It was at that time, when Dahlia was again trying to increase her income, that she kept getting calls from Butri, a relative of hers from back home. Thinking that Butri might be able to help find her a better job, she went over to see her as Butri had asked.

She wasn't the same after that fatal misstep. She withdrew into herself and didn't talk to her co-workers unless she absolutely had to. She didn't feel like the same woman anymore, and she thought about just ending it all—but what about her parents and her brother? She had to make more money, she had to help ease her family's burdens. Then one day, she saw an ad in the paper for a place that was hiring hostesses. It was a club, and they were looking for young, attractive women, in good shape, with a middle or high school education. The ad said you could earn upwards of three thousand a month, that there were commissions for good earners, and that they even provided meals. To a girl like her, this was an offer too good to be true, and Dahlia was spellbound by its promise. She signed up without a second thought.

2

A LOT OF GIRLS HAD RESPONDED TO THE AD, BUT UNLIKE WHAT it said in the paper, the lady in charge didn't ask for any high school diplomas; she inspected their figures, their features, their postures, then picked twenty of the best. At first Dahlia was worried that she'd lost her shot at getting better money, but before it was over, she'd made the cut. The boss gathered up the girls and told them that they were in luck—they'd be working at a place called the Rose, but they had to work hard. Their futures were full of promise, she added, and each of them first had to put down a two-thousand-yuan deposit. Dahlia and a few of the girls like her had no way to pay such an amount and were on the verge of leaving when the boss whipped out the contracts bearing their fingerprints and waved them coldly before their eyes. "You can't just up and leave like that, I'm afraid," she announced sternly, "this is a legally binding contract." When they'd first arrived that day, the girls had all been in a rush to fill out the form as requested. Giddy with the prospect of getting the job, they'd signed the contract and even put their fingerprints on it without stopping to read the fine print. Now, without quite knowing how, they owed the boss a two-thousand-yuan deposit, and they had nowhere to run. Dahlia had no choice but to work off her debt.

When the boss started teaching them how to smoke, how to walk in high heels—even how to shake their asses—they finally realized they'd been had.

Dahlia would never have done such a sordid job in the past, even if it were a matter of life and death, but ever since that cursed snowy winter's night when the cold-blooded Karma Dorjé had defiled her body and laid waste to her gentle spirit, ideas like self-respect and self-esteem didn't seem to be relevant to her anymore, so she accepted the Rose's conditions without putting up a fight. But her brother idolized his sister and her parents adored their daughter, and if they were to find out, there was a real danger that her brother would drop out of school to return home, and her parents would surely have a nervous breakdown. Every time she thought of this, it felt as though her heart was being chopped to pieces. In the end, Dahlia decided that she would have to do it for now, just for the money, and when her brother had finished university, she would get out of that dark world no matter what. She reluctantly began working at the club, setting her sights on the day of her brother's graduation.

At the Rose, Dahlia relied on her sweet smile and her skilful flattery to increase her income. She gave her precious body to others, in a manner that was unwilling, unfeeling, and entirely joyless, all for the sake of making money. Over time she grew to accept the work. To Dahlia, the parents who had given her life and the brother who was bound to her by blood were everything. It was unacceptable for them to face destitution, and so she came to value money more than her own life. By her second year at the Rose, not only was her family able to fix up their unfinished home, they affixed white tiles to the walls, making their house one of the best in the village. For the first time in a long time, her parents found themselves smiling and they were able to hold their heads up in the community.

Time moved unstoppably forward, but Dahlia's work remained the same as always. The Rose's fortunes in business waxed and waned and there were several turnovers in ownership, but the club never went under, and the customers never stopped coming. As before, Dahlia relied on her sweet smile and her skilful flattery to make money. But at a certain point, she began to feel weak and she lost her appetite. Before, she could really handle her drink and keep up with all the toasts, and her income kept rising as a result. But now she had grown to loathe drinking and she avoided the toasts as much as possible. From out of nowhere, her whole body started to feel tired like never before, and when the clients requested those extra services, she felt completely unwilling and simply incapable of doing it.

3

ONE SUMMER NIGHT, DAHLIA PUT ON HER MAKEUP, GOT DRESSED, and went to work, but she hadn't the will to serve her customers, much less the energy, and all she could do was sit on a bench in the main hall of the club, trying to gather her strength. She was sweating all over and her clothes were sticking to her, so she decided to take the night off. She made her way out of the club with heavy steps, and when she came to the front door, she noticed a teenager pacing back and forth outside. Curious, she stopped in her tracks and leaned against a wall by the entrance, where she continued to peek at him. She barely had to look to know what he was after.

"Hey kid, you waiting for someone?" she called to him.

"Oh, yeah, I'm waiting for someone," he mumbled, bashfully checking his surroundings.

"Is it me you're waiting for?"

He looked at her in astonishment, as if to say, How did you know?

"You've been out here for a while right? I think I know who you're waiting for. But have you got this?" She rubbed her thumb over her index and middle fingers. "There's no such thing as a free lunch."

"Yes I do," he replied immediately. "Let's get a taxi and go to a hotel."

They went to a mid-range hotel, and when the kid shut the door of their room, he instantly adopted an authoritative air. He went to the fridge, took out a can of beer and downed it one go, then planted himself on the sofa like a businessman would, his previously awkward demeanour now nowhere to be seen.

"How old are you?" she asked, eyeing him. The kid seemed unconcerned.

"Old enough, don't ask me about that. Achak, if you stay with me for two nights, I'll pay you one thousand yuan," he said, no hesitation at all. "What?" said the kid, seeing her surprised reaction. "You don't think I'm good for it? You don't need to worry about money. Money's no problem for me. I'll even pay for all your meals." He nonchalantly counted off ten hundred-yuan bills and handed them to her. "My mum and dad have gone off to China for the new year. It's only me and the maid at home. It gets lonely by myself, to tell you the truth, so I came out for a bit of fun. I'll call the maid and tell her I'm staying at a classmate's house."

"You didn't go to China to spend new year with your family?" she asked, surprised.

He scoffed. "Ha, my mum went with a man who isn't my dad, and my dad went with a woman who isn't my mum. You tell me, which one am I supposed to go with? Don't ask me about that stuff. I don't want to talk about it. Just thinking about it makes me upset." His voice had lowered, and without her noticing exactly when, his bright eyes had started to well up. At that moment the room felt very still.

Dahlia wanted to console or offer some advice to the kid sitting before her, but she didn't know what to say. She thought of her little brother. This teenager had whipped out a stack of hundreds without batting an eyelid just for the sake of entertainment, but that same amount of money would support her brother for two whole months. She felt like crying, and at the same time, she suddenly felt surprisingly sorry for the kid. Unlike those dirty men who came to the Rose, he actually treated her as a woman.

"Achak," he said, looking straight at her, "you're so pretty." He kissed her once on the forehead, innocently. She felt strangely moved. She'd been with so many men, kissed countless men, and had been kissed unfeelingly more times than she could count. But every one of those kisses was simply a financial transaction—none of those men had ever seen her as a real woman or kissed her out of genuine affection. The boy's kiss brought a faint ray of warmth to her heart.

He wanted her, but not in the same way as those degenerates who went to the Union Hotel. He treated Dahlia as a woman, and he tried to satisfy his desires considerately and without being smutty. Dahlia, for her part, did her best to give him what he wanted. During the day he spent most of his time playing games on his phone, and Dahlia could just lie around, eating and relaxing.

Before they parted ways, he said, "Achak, give me your phone number, then I can call you whenever I miss you. This whole thing—it's just between us, no one else needs to know. You should get a cab and head home."

Before she left, Dahlia took out the one thousand yuan he'd given her and stuffed it into his hand. "Boy, I know that money's of no concern for you. But you should look after yourself, and don't go doing this sort of thing again. You're young and your family is well off. You should study hard, get a good job, and in the future you should start a family, have kids, and live a good, honest life. You've got a beautiful, promising future ahead of you. I won't give you my phone number."

"I know, Achak, I know," said the kid impatiently, apparently not wanting to hear the advice. He tried to give the money back to Dahlia, but she pushed his hand away insistently. "OK fine, but take this for the taxi," he said, handing her one of the notes.

Dahlia took the elevator down, wondering to herself why she had felt the need to treat a complete stranger this way, why she had given the money back. *I really need the money, especially now that I'm not feeling good. But I…* she walked the busy streets, going over things in her head. She ate a bit of breakfast then went back to the apartment to sleep.

She had the place to herself that night, but she lay in the silent room unable to fall asleep, tormented all night long by a fever and a thirst so bad her lips cracked. Ever since she'd come to Lhasa she'd never had a problem sleeping at night—no matter what her troubles during the day—and now she was discovering how long a sleepless night could be. The girls trickled back in one after another around dawn and went straight to bed completely exhausted, none of them paying any attention to her. Despite the fact that Dahlia was burning up, when Azalea got in bed she was so tired she just turned over, not saying a word to her, and went out like a light. Dahlia now felt even more uncomfortable in the narrow bed, but she didn't dare move too much for fear of waking Azalea.

She fell asleep as the rosy light of the morning clouds was coming in through the window. Around noon, when it was time to eat, the other girls got up one by one. Dahlia was completely awake by that point, but she showed no sign of getting out of bed. Before she went to wash up, Azalea threw back the duvet and said, "It's time to get up, lazybones! Come on, up you get. Where have you been anyway? Tell me, no secrets allowed." Dahlia said nothing, and she still showed no sign of getting up. "Achak, don't just lie there," said Azalea insistently, pulling the duvet off completely. "Let's go get something to eat." Dahlia yanked the duvet back up and wouldn't budge an inch. Magnolia and Cassia, unwilling to wait around for her, went out to eat. Azalea twisted her lip in disapproval. "You're a pain, Achak. We only get two meals a day, you can't skip one of them. I'll wait for you, hurry up and get ready."

"Yangdzom, I've not being feeling well recently," said Dahlia. "I had a fever all night and couldn't sleep. I'm completely exhausted. I don't feel like doing a thing today except crying." Two big tears fell from her almond-shaped eyes onto her cheeks. She wiped them off with difficulty, then turned her head away.

Azalea touched the back of her hand to Dahlia's brow and

realized she really was burning up. "Achak Drölkar," she said, nervous now, "I thought you weren't looking well recently, and you've lost so much weight. We have to take you to see a doctor."

"I don't feel good down there, it really hurts. I think I might have caught something. I know it's a risk with this job, but I always thought it'd be OK as long as we were safe. But it's got worse today. It's swelling, and itchy, and it hurts really bad. And there's this horrible smell, like something rotting. It's a bad sign." She started weeping disconsolately.

Azalea wiped away her tears. "You just look a bit unwell, is all. Don't think like that. Let's pray on the Three Jewels that it's nothing that serious."

Dahlia sighed deeply, not at all comforted. "My brother hasn't finished school yet. If I've got a disease like that, I'll have no way to get money for him. What am I going to do?" Tears welled up once more in her bright, round eyes, and now Azalea, too, was crying.

"Achak Drölkar, maybe our karma is catching up with us after everything we've done in this life. But I never thought we'd get punished so fast. The best thing we can do right now is go see a doctor, so let's get you to the hospital." She hugged Dahlia, then tried to get her up, but Dahlia shook her head.

"I can't go to the hospital like this, not today. Just pretend for now that you don't know. I'll tell the Rose that I've caught a cold and need to take a few days off, then I can go to the hospital." Azalea kept on pleading with her to go now, but it was no use.

Dahlia lay in bed, anguished, feeling like her heart was cracked to pieces. She wasn't surprised that she'd got sick like this. If she couldn't recover from it there was no way she could keep working, and even if she did continue with that miserable job for the sake of survival, she'd just be adding to her sins. She suddenly thought of the teenager. If they'd swapped phone numbers, she'd have a way to get in touch now and tell him he needed to go see a doctor to get tested. But how could she contact him now? Lhasa is so huge, how could she possibly track him down? All she could do now was repent and pray that the Three Jewels watched over him and made sure he came to no harm.

She had no choice: she had to get medical help. After a long internal struggle, she got up the next morning and went to the hospital. Since it was still early when she set out, the other three were all sound asleep. Before she left, Dahlia glanced at Azalea's face. She was sleeping peacefully that morning, and Dahlia thought again of that awful night and how she'd led this poor girl down the wrong path. *What will we do if she ends up getting sick like me?* Plagued by guilt, she didn't dare think about it anymore. Wiping away her tears, she opened the door softly and set off for the hospital.

4

"DRÖLKAR, DRÖLKAR, DRÖLKAR." THE NURSE CALLED HER NAME quietly at first, then yelled it three times. The nurse's shouts hushed the chatter of the patients waiting in the corridor. They all sat on the bench, waiting and looking around, denying that they were Drölkar with their blank expressions.

The moment of quiet that punctuated the usual clamour of the hospital corridor caused Dahlia to snap out of her daydreaming. Realizing that the nurse's shouts of "Drölkar" referred to her, she jumped up in a fluster and was about to answer when the nurse called someone else. Ever since she started at the Rose, no one had called her by her name except Azalea. Her ID card and her residence permit still bore that name, but otherwise she was Dahlia now. Even when she collected her paycheck at the club, she signed her name as Dahlia.

When the other patient came back out of the room, she rushed in. "Doctor, I'm so sorry, my mind was elsewhere just now and I didn't hear my name being called. I'm Drölkar." She bowed her head slightly and smiled sheepishly. The hospital's examination rooms were completely different from the corridor outside. When the door closed, a brightly lit, white world appeared before her eyes. The equipment in the room was simple, but everything was spotlessly clean. A sweet smell that she couldn't identify pervaded the room and drifted up to her nostrils; it was a hospital smell, completely unlike the smell of makeup, cigarettes, and alcohol.

The doctor had her head down and was writing something in her chart. Dahlia could only see part of her face, but her singular feminine elegance was immediately apparent: her neatly parted hair hung over her long neck, slender like a vase, and her soft, white hands darted nimbly over the clipboard. When she'd finished writing her notes she rose and washed her hands, then sat back on her stool and turned her attention to Dahlia.

"What brings you in today?" She sounded just like Isaura the slave girl, the main character from a Brazilian TV series she'd seen when she was at primary school. The doctor's soft, warm voice and her slim, elegant bearing made Dahlia think of that poetic metaphor she'd learned in high school—"A figure like bamboo from Tsari, a voice like the song of a nightingale"—a couplet that almost seemed to have been written just for this woman.

Though Dahlia had seen many girls at the Rose who were younger and prettier than the doctor, most of them had been nipped and tucked and concealed their natural looks under layers of makeup. The doctor had made a very favourable impression on her.

"What seems to be the problem, my dear?" The doctor, noticing Dahlia's distraction, gently repeated her question. Dahlia gathered herself, but could only stutter awkwardly. She indicated her crotch with her hand, too embarrassed to say it out loud.

"OK, please remove your trousers and lie down on the bed," said the doctor, not fazed in the least.

"I have to take off my trousers, doctor?" said Dahlia, thinking she might have misheard her.

"Well, you're here for an exam, aren't you?" the doctor replied offhandedly.

Dahlia had got undressed in front of countless men, baring her body without a second thought, yet the thought of taking off her trousers in front of this female doctor filled her with embarrassment. Forcing herself to get over it, she slowly undid her belt and did what the doctor told her. The doctor donned a pair of medical gloves and inspected her crotch.

"Why didn't you come in for this sooner, child? Your vagina is severely inflamed. If you don't get this treated immediately, you're putting yourself at great risk." The doctor had her get down from the bed and began scribbling on her chart. "First we need to run bloodwork and get a urine sample. You've contracted an STI— probably syphilis. It's important to watch your hygiene—and your conduct."

The doctor handed her some forms. At that moment all she could think was *It's finished, everything's finished.* Everything before her eyes went as black as night, and the doctor's words echoed over and over in her ears—*probably syphilis probably syphilis.* After a moment she came back to her senses. *It's clear what it is. I don't want to hear it. She's given me the prognosis, so why waste money on pointless tests?*

"Doctor," she said faintly, almost begging, "I'm really busy with work at the minute. Could you just give me something for the inflammation first? I can come back in when I've got more time."

The doctor was stunned. "Honestly, you young people these days. Won't listen to what's good for you. But I take my responsibilities as a doctor very seriously, and I'm telling you now—you need the tests, and you need to get this treated." The doctor's tone was forceful, even commanding.

Her words left Dahlia feeling even more uncomfortable, and all she could do was stammer in response. The doctor continued, more gently now, as though she understood her burdens.

"The reason I'm being so blunt is that this isn't a common gynaecological condition. There are different types of syphilis, and if it's the kind that's hard to treat, then that's a problem. And if you don't get it treated right away, you're putting your life at serious risk. I cannot stress this enough: it's vital that you do not have sexual intercourse with your husband at this time. Right now the bacteria is multiplying and there is a high risk of you passing it on to others. If the results of the tests show that it's still in the early stages, then things will be easier. Of course, I'm hoping that that's the case."

Dahlia's terror grew. *What if it really is the kind that can't be treated? Then that piece of paper with the test results will be my death sentence. In the last few years I've only ever had the odd flu, and I've never been to the hospital before. Now I set foot in one for the first time and it turns out I've got a terrible disease like this!* She shrank back, not daring to take the test form. The doctor thrusted it into her hands. "Do you have children?" she asked, going to the sink to wash her hands again.

Dahlia held the form in her hands, trembling. "No, how could I, I'm not even married yet," she said, her voice quivering. The doctor said nothing, she just shook her head and sighed. She turned back to face Dahlia.

"Dear, you must do the tests. The quicker we determine what it is, the easier it will be to treat. Time waits for no one."

Dahlia left the room clutching the form tightly, tears of despair in her eyes. She drifted listlessly out on to the street, as though she had already accepted the worst. She walked, shedding bitter tears, every now and then becoming aware of the sound of her own crying. *How can a woman be whole when she has a disease like this? And a woman like me really can't afford to be messed up down there, not with my damn job. My body is my gold, my loins are my silver—how can I survive without them? Who'll pay for Dad's medicine? Who'll support my brother?* Dahlia's heart was close to breaking and everything before her was fuzzy. She slumped down on a bench by the side of the road, the doctor's words ringing in her ears again. Unable to escape her thoughts, the tears came back like a fountain. No matter how hard she tried to push down the pain, she couldn't hold it in. She rolled off the bench and knelt on the ground, clutching at her hair and howling uncontrollably. The passers-by swarmed past, each on their own paths and going about their own business, not paying the slightest bit of attention to her.

After a while, Dahlia had cried herself hoarse, and she fell still, watching the people streaming past. *If someone like me died right here on the street, this city wouldn't shed a single tear. That's the difference between the city and the country. But I'm still young. I can't just throw my life away. I must get treatment, I must get better. I need to get it together, at least until Tsering finishes school.* She dragged herself up off the ground and headed home.

When the girls got out of bed that day, there was no sign of Dahlia and her phone was switched off, so the three of them stayed in the room and waited for her. When Azalea heard the sound of heavy footsteps on the stairway, she knew right away it was her, and she rushed out of the room loudly airing her grievances.

"What's the matter with you, Achak, going out on your own and not even waking us up? It's past noon already and your phone's off. I've been worried sick! Where on earth have you been?"

Dahlia didn't answer. She looked weak and pale, the fact that she hadn't put makeup on that morning only adding to her sickly appearance. Her unusual manner made Azalea nervous. She tugged at Dahlia's hand, but still got no response. Dahlia, as though all these words were meant for someone else, brushed past Azalea and into the room without so much as a glance. She tossed her handbag onto the bed, exhaled deeply, then crawled under the covers and just lay there, staring blankly at the ceiling. The girls were all worried now, and they crowded around Dahlia's bed.

"Achak, has someone done something to you?"

"Is it your family? Are they OK?" said Magnolia.

The girls peppered her with anxious questions, but Dahlia just kept lying there, not saying a word. They had no choice but to wait, their imaginations running wild trying to figure out what had happened to her. They brought food and water to her bedside, not knowing what else to do, but Dahlia didn't react at all. Azalea thought that her illness must have taken a turn for the worse, but all she could do was sigh to herself and cry.

Dahlia lay there for two whole days, not eating, not drinking, not speaking. After an excruciating fourty-eight hours, Dahlia finally dragged herself out of bed. But her complexion was now even paler, her pretty eyes were sunken, and her body was so weak she could barely support herself. As she got up, a crumpled-up piece of paper fell to the floor—it was the bloodwork form given to her by the doctor. Azalea picked up the paper and looked at it, but all she saw was a jumble of Chinese characters that she couldn't read. The doctor's handwriting just looked to her like a bunch of crooked, unintelligible scribbles. She started to panic.

"Achak, what is it, what did the doctor say? You've been lying there completely silent for two whole days. Even if there's nothing we can do to help, you can still talk things over with us, get some advice. You've got me worried to death."

Magnolia approached her bedside. Smoothing down her tussled hair, she said, "Dahlia, no matter what your burdens, no matter what your problems, you can't keep it all bottled up inside like this. We sisters all have the same karma, and that's why we came together here. Please, you have to tell us what's wrong." It was no use—Dahlia still wouldn't answer.

Cassia didn't really know Tibetan, but she nodded her head as though she'd understood every word Magnolia had said and poured a cup of hot water for Dahlia. Dahlia put the cup that Cassia handed her back on the table. She remained as silent as before, but two streams of tears now ran in parallel lines down her cheeks and into the edges of her mouth. Dahlia's pitiful appearance made the others shudder with a cold chill. The room fell completely silent, no one talking now. Dahlia wanted to say something to her sisters, but nothing came out. Azalea was tormented inside, and it even felt hard to breathe, but she pushed it all down, trying not to let her inner feelings show. She went to sit beside Dahlia.

"Achak, please talk to us. What did the doctor say?" Dahlia

pressed her lips tight shut, giving no answer, and Azalea stroked her cheek anxiously. "Look, you're so thin these days, and you're white as a sheet. Why don't you take some time off and rest, put everything else out of your mind? We'll go out this afternoon and try to find a better place for us. We'll buy some things to cook with and we can make food ourselves at home. I became quite the chef when I was at Mr. Nyendrak's place. I can whip you up some real nice things, you'll see."

Finally, Dahlia spoke. "Money is everything to me now," she said faintly. "I don't want to waste a single penny. If it's really syphilis like the doctor said, then there's nothing left I can do but go rob a bank."

When Azalea heard this, her face fell and she was struck dumb for a moment, unable to believe her ears. "Achak," she said suddenly, as though she'd just thought of something, "don't be so worried. No matter what it is you've got, there'll surely be a way to treat it. With all the technology they've got these days, the only thing they can't cure is cancer."

Magnolia, too, couldn't believe what she had heard at first, and it took a moment for her to compose herself. "What sister Azalea says is true. Don't be so down. Lots of people we know get this illness, and when they're cured, they come right back to work. The hospitals are so amazing these days, you'll definitely get better." Magnolia spoke rapidly, sounding positive, but inside she was terrified: *What if Dahlia's fate today is mine tomorrow?* Magnolia, who was normally such a smooth talker, could think of no further consolation to offer. Meanwhile, all of this had left Cassia with a curious expression on her face. Though she couldn't speak Tibetan, she could understand a little bit. The majority of their conversation had gone over her head, but she knew at least that Dahlia had a serious illness. She looked at Dahlia closely then turned to Azalea to ask what the matter was, but Azalea just shook her head and said nothing.

"Elder sister," she whispered to Magnolia deferentially, "what is it that our Achak Dahlia has?"

Magnolia, losing her temper, answered back in Chinese. "I don't know! Mind your own business!" Cassia looked at the ground, afraid, not knowing what else to say. A moment later she jumped up off the corner of Dahlia's bed as though something had just occurred to her, then hurriedly brushed down her backside and went to sit on her own bed.

Azalea had no parents now, no relatives, no one in the world except for Dahlia. She hugged her tightly and the two of them cried together for a long time. Magnolia and Cassia cried too—it was the only way they had to show their sympathy.

Azalea knew that the burden of making money was now on her shoulders alone. She tried again to console her. "Achak, even if there's only the tiniest hope, you can't give up, you have to get the treatment. I'll get more work, make more money." She went down to the street and bought a bowl of chicken soup, which she made Dahlia eat. Dahlia had no appetite at all, she didn't want so much as a drop of water, but she ate the soup to put Azalea's mind at ease. Now that she finally had some hot food in her, she felt a warmth spread throughout her body, her mind became a bit clearer, and, slowly, she was able to get up. With Dahlia out of bed, the others felt some relief, and they went off to work. Dahlia was left alone in the room, and everything was quiet. She thought of her brother. She wanted to call him, but after thinking about it for a moment, she decided that she couldn't express her feelings over the phone, so she wrote a letter instead. She sat up in bed, rested a piece of paper on her knees, and started writing.

My dear brother,

I know from the phone call the other day that all is well with you, so I'm not worried at all. But for some reason, I suddenly really missed you today. I must have good karma from a past life for us two to be brother and sister in this one. Wouldn't it be nice if a family never had to be separated—and even if we did have to be apart, wouldn't it be wonderful if we could be reunited in the next life?

Tsering, my dear brother, I have so many things I want to say right now, but I don't know where to start. What should I do? I wish I had a pair of wings so I could fly to you. If there is a next life, I'd want to be your sister again.

By the time she'd written this far, the tears were streaming down her face and dripping onto the paper in her hands. When she became aware of it, she steeled herself, then diverted the little black letters away from her inner pain and onto other subjects.

Even though you got into a top-class school in Beijing all through your own hard work, you've had to struggle to get by because of your family's financial circumstances. But your big sister got a promotion at the company, and now I'm on a monthly salary of four thousand yuan as the head of a whole department, so starting next month I'll be sending one thousand yuan a month for your living costs. You're still a growing lad and it's very important that you eat well—even if you can't have the healthiest diet, you've got to make sure you eat enough. My biggest worry is that you're coming up on your fourth year of college this year and you still don't have your own computer. I'm putting six thousand yuan in your account. Take four thousand and spend it on a good laptop and use the rest to pay for your meals and to get yourself some new clothes. Now that there are direct trains, most students off in the east come home for the holidays, and they do cheap student tickets as well, so I want you to come home this winter. I'll try to think of a way to get back too. I don't need to say anything else. You're a good, hard-working kid and you know what you're doing. The one piece of advice I have is this: take good care of your health. That's all for now.

Hoping that we see each other soon.

From Lhasa, City of the Gods
Your sister
--th of the --th month, 20--

She put the letter in an envelope, affixed a stamp, then touched the envelope to her forehead and gave it a kiss. She felt like she had accomplished something very important. Still, she missed her brother, and a couple of stray tears fell on the envelope, dampening it. She wiped the envelope with hands so emaciated they looked like chicken feet, then placed it on the table. She leaned back in bed again, and with slow, pained movements, took her phone from her bag and dialled the number for home. When she heard the familiar voice of her mother on the other end of the line, her eyes welled up again.

"Hi, hello? My daughter, is that you? You haven't called in so long! Sometimes I miss you so much and I want to call you, but I'm still not so good with these phones, and I'm always worried about bothering you at work."

"I'm fine Mum, don't worry. I've been thinking about you and Dad a lot these past couple of days. Sometimes I even dream about coming home. I can't at the minute with things so busy at work, but I'll come when things calm down, I promise. I'm giving Dorjé from the village some money to bring back to you for the fertilizer and for Dad's medicine, plus a bit extra for you to get some tea. Take good care of yourself, Mum." By this point, she was choked with tears, and couldn't go on.

"I know you're busy, love. But you've got to look after yourself. We don't even dare think about what would happen to this family without you. People are never satisfied with what they've got these days, that's what I reckon, so don't be too hard on yourself. No matter how good you have it somewhere else, there's still no place like home. You'll always have a loving home to come back to here. If you want to come back then take a few days off and come home. We're all alone here now without our kids. Your dad and I miss you and your brother very much." She stopped there, and for a while no sound came from the other end of the line.

Dahlia listened silently, not knowing how to respond. Her mother, trying to conceal her feelings, wiped the tears from her cheeks with rugged, dirt-encrusted hands and continued with feigned cheeriness. "I'm doing well, anyway, dear. Your dad's getting his medicine, thanks to you, and he's doing better now. We've added four hens and two roosters this year, and the sow's about to give birth, too. If we sell them, we can send some money to your brother. That way we can take a bit of the burden off you." Right when Dahlia's mother was in the middle of updating her on the family situation, her dad snatched the phone from her hands.

"It'll cost us a fortune, being on the phone for this long!" he said. He clutched the phone tightly, held it close to his mouth, and shouted, "Don't you worry about us, daughter, we're doing just fine. You've got to rely on yourself when you're away from home, so you be careful. And you'd better be home for Losar this year— it's been four years since you went away! Your mother and me miss you both. Right, if there's nothing else, let's leave it there for today. Be sure to look after yourself!" He hung up the phone abruptly with a click.

Dahlia felt weak that day. She didn't want to move or speak, but when she heard her parents' voices, she felt suddenly revitalized. She thought of the mountains and valleys of home, of the fields and the cool, clear streams, the sweet songs sung by the shepherds. She wanted her parents to tell her more about home, but she no longer heard those voices from the phone, just the monotonous tone of a disconnected line. With a last glance at her phone, she hung up the call, and gently laid it aside. She rolled over and lay on the bed, recounting in her mind everything her parents had said just now. They'd been trying to suppress their true feelings, but deep lines of longing now marked their features, and it was clear from their trembling voices that, though they were separated by countless mountains and valleys, they couldn't hide the profound affection they felt for their daughter. Her mind was carried off to her distant homeland like a feather on the wind, and her loving parents and the little valley where she'd grown up appeared vividly before her eyes, just like she was watching a movie, and in that instant, she felt a powerful urge to return home. But the fantasy only lasted a moment.

I can't go home now. I have to make money for my brother, for my family. Besides, what else am I qualified to do but this? We might have land at home, but I don't know how to farm anymore. And anyway, this job might not be great, but it lets me wear nice clothes, and when I'm with the clients I can eat all the finest foods, I can smoke the best cigarettes and drink expensive booze—if I had to give up this life just like that, well, I don't know if I could. And now that I'm sick, I really need the money. Doesn't matter if I want to or not, doesn't matter if I love it or hate it, I just have to keep working.

But I need to think about others as well. Absolutely no more special services from now on. I'll just have to get by on my sweet smile and those feminine charms to make my money.

She made this promise to herself as though she were carving it into a rock.

A few days later, she was feeling a little better, so she put on her makeup and went to work. Dahlia made her money by serving the clients with her usual seductive guile and suggestive winks, but before long the weakness came back and she wasn't even capable of showing a fake smile to the customers, leaving her with no choice but to take time off again and go back to the hospital.

Dahlia and Azalea first went to a small private clinic because it was cheaper and more convenient, but the doctor there told them, "For this condition, we can only give you a drip to reduce the inflammation. There's not much else we can do. You have to go to a proper hospital." Dahlia promised she would do as the doctor said, but first asked them to put her on an IV for a few days, after which she showed clear signs of improvement. Following the doctor's recommendation, she bought a good supply of antibiotics from the little clinic, and after a couple of weeks of resting and taking the medicine, she recovered her strength, she felt no discomfort in her vagina, and it seemed like her body was back to normal. Though she thought often of what that elegant doctor had said the first time she went to hospital, if she just stayed at home recuperating all the time, who'd make money for her family? Who'd send money to her brother? Ever since that first day that Dahlia went to the hospital, these questions had stuck to her, like a shadow to a body. Once again, Dahlia powdered her face, put on her lipstick, sprayed herself with perfume, and went off with the others to work. But since she was declining to offer those special services, there was a noticeable drop in her income. She valued money like her life now, so she grasped every opportunity to make the money she needed: she flashed her white teeth and her ruby red lips, numbly handing over every part of herself to the ugly, foul-breathed customers, letting them grope any part of her body they liked. But it wasn't long before the sickness came back. Things were deteriorating by the day: her whole body was burning up, she became thinner and thinner until she was nothing but skin and bones, her complexion grew increasingly sickly, and dark rashes had emerged on her skin. Worst of all, not only could she smell a putrid odour drifting up from her groin, the people around her could smell it too.

Dahlia didn't have the energy to serve the clients anymore and she was forced to stop doing the only thing that could make her money. Before, her condition was known only to the girls she lived with, but now everyone at the Rose could see there was something wrong. Everyone advised her to go to the doctor, and meanwhile, they began to keep their distance. It was only her roommates, her sisters, who really cared for her now. They, too, urged her to go to the hospital, but Dahlia was terrified and didn't dare. "If I check into the hospital, I won't check out," she kept saying. She put it off again and again, until her sisters were sick with worry and at a complete loss. Dahlia had it her way and spent all day in the room by herself resting, but all she was really resting was her body— inside, she was so worried she felt like she might go crazy.

One day, it was just her and Cassia in the room. Cassia was rummaging through Azalea and Magnolia's clothes, looking for something to wear. Since Dahlia wasn't going to work now, she wasn't really fussy about her clothes anymore. Slowly pulling herself up, she retrieved her suitcase from under the bed, then took out a pretty blouse and handed it to Cassia.

"Here, I don't have much use for this anymore, why don't you wear it."

Cassia, who was normally so fond of borrowing her sister's clothes, became fidgety and pulled a strange face. She pushed away the shirt in Dahlia's outstretched hands.

"Achak, how could I possibly take such an expensive thing of yours." It was as though Cassia, who normally had no compunctions about such things, had suddenly acquired some principles. Realizing that her words had hurt Dahlia, she felt awkward, and went to pour her a glass of hot water. "Don't be sad, Achak. There's no illness that doesn't go away with treatment," she said in an effort to comfort her. She fetched a clean cup and poured some water for herself. Cassia was always drinking from the other girl's cups—she didn't even own one of her own—and it was obvious that she was worried about catching Dahlia's disease. When Dahlia saw this she felt the anger well up inside. She wanted to say something, but she swallowed her words and held her peace. She put the cup of water back on the table, turned her back to Cassia, then pulled the duvet up over her head and lay there silently.

Azalea came home shortly after. She called Dahlia's name but got no reply. When she pulled back the duvet, she saw that she was crying. Thinking that her illness must have taken a turn for the worse, she touched her hand to Dahlia's forehead and found that she was burning up. She ripped off the covers. "Are you going to just die like this, lying here in an empty room all by yourself? You have to go to the hospital, right now!" Driven by Azalea's relentless insistence, she got unsteadily to her feet and agreed to go to the hospital. As they were heading out the door, Cassia came over to support her, but Dahlia raised a hand, not wanting to let her touch her. Cassia felt ashamed at having so carelessly hurt her sister's feelings, and she stayed behind, watching with remorse as they disappeared into the alleyway.

When they got to the entrance of the hospital, Dahlia spoke to her friend as though she were issuing an order. "Yangdzom, with the Three Jewels as my witness, I will check myself in and get treatment, but you can't come with me. If anyone sees you, they might think you've caught the disease as well, and I can't let you come to any more harm on my account. Wait outside the hospital for me." After Azalea had seen her inside, she went to a teahouse next door and waited.

This was the same hospital she'd been to before, and the doctor was also the same one from before. After waiting in the corridor for what seemed like an age, a nurse finally emerged and called her name. She shuffled inside.

"Doctor," she said meekly, "I've been feeling feverish for a while now, and it won't go away. And in the last few days my mouth has got really dry and my lips are cracked."

Perhaps the doctor hadn't heard her, or perhaps she thought such an explanation was superfluous, but she paid no attention at all to what Dahlia said and once again handed her the form for bloodwork and a urine sample—the exact same one as before. There weren't many patients that day, so she was soon back before the doctor with the test results in hand. The doctor looked carefully at the piece of paper, then shook her head in disappointment.

"Yes. I was very clear with you before about the serious nature of this illness, but you chose not to listen to me. Why do so many patients these days disregard their doctor's advice? This disease is referred to as syphilis in medical texts, but there are four different types of it. Your condition has already progressed to stage three, so the best thing for you now is to be hospitalized for immediate treatment. This is not an easy thing to recover from, and the expenses will be considerable. A full recovery is unlikely, and it is even more unlikely that you will be able to conceive in the future." The doctor wrote out her hospitalization forms with an air of finality.

"Doctor," said Dahlia, her voice shaking, "I'm a hostess at a bar, I can't afford the treatment. But I need to get better as fast as possible." The doctor eyed her simple but elegant clothes and her prettily made up face, as though she couldn't believe that a prostitute could clean up so nice. Dahlia had an idea of what she was thinking.

"Doctor, we're people in the day and demons at night. People like us look different depending on the time of day."

The doctor didn't respond to this, but sighed deeply, unable to hide her sympathy for Dahlia.

"But dear, money isn't everything. Your life is extremely precious."

Dahlia's expression was frightful and hopeless now. "You're right, doctor, money isn't everything in life, but it can still save lives. But…" her tears cut her off.

The doctor sat in silence for a moment, then looked into Dahlia's eyes with deep compassion. "I'm not asking what it is you do, dear," she said softly. "You're my patient, and that's all I need to know. What can be more important than your life? Don't let it go. Even if there's only the tiniest thread of hope, we have to hold on to it tightly." She placed the hospitalization forms into Dahlia's hands.

"I'm going to die anyway," said Dahlia, in tears, "staying in the hospital is just a waste of money. I'm better off making the most of the time I have left and getting as much as money as I can for my brother and my family."

The doctor said nothing to this.

"Have you been sleeping well recently?" she asked after a moment. "Or do you feel as if you're hearing things, seeing things?"

"I lie in bed awake a lot of the time. I'm always seeing life at the Rose, all the people there and the hustle and bustle, or imagining my brother finishing school and getting a job then coming to bring me the good news. It feels like I'm actually hearing their voices."

"Those are hallucinations. It's a sign that your condition is deteriorating. You must be hospitalized."

Five

1

XIAO LI WAS FROM A VILLAGE IN SICHUAN. FOR THE FAMILIES there, income from farming was just enough to cover the bare necessities. It left no money to spare, so most of the able-bodied young men and women left the fields of Sichuan and headed for the cities to find work. When these young workers returned home at the end of the year, they brought with them tens of thousands in earnings that transformed their families' fortunes, enabling them to build new houses and buy new furniture. Year after year, the mass exodus of young men and women leaving their little valley and heading to the cities for work got more and more severe, until there were only a handful of people left in the village.

The soil on her land was fertile and they received plenty of rain, so they could grow an abundance of grains, fruits, and vegetables, but this was still only enough for subsistence living—there was no way they could get rich off the land. Most families with the means to do so rented out land on the cheap, and if no one rented it, they let it lie fallow. All the able-bodied laborers left to make money, and those families who could afford it had left for the cities themselves, leaving their land and homes in the hands of relatives.

Journalists from Sichuan and from China Central Television came and filmed an investigative report about how the farmers were neglecting their land and weren't planting crops. The villagers had never really put much thought into the problem before, but when they saw the report on TV, they realized there really were only a handful of people left in the village. Three of them were women, six were children, and nine were old folks. But still they didn't pay much mind to the problem, thinking only of the profits that lay ahead. All of the adults had the same goal and the same dream: make money, enough to build a house, enough to send their kids to college, then they could live out their remaining years at home in peace and quiet.

For a time, Xiao Li's family consisted of no more than her father and her stepmother, then after a few years, her stepmother gave birth to a baby boy. From that point on, her stepbrother was the apple of their eye, and her parents decided that it was essential for the boy's future that he get an education and then land a stable and lucrative government job. By that time, she had just graduated from middle school, but her stepmother, on the pretext that their family was in a bad financial state, said that she couldn't continue her schooling and had to head off to make money for the family. Her father couldn't bear to do things this way, so he took his daughter's place and went off to Shanghai to find work. Without her dad at home, her stepmother treated Xiao Li as even more of a thorn in her side, and her unappeasable wrath now came out in the open. When they were eating, she would always berate and curse her for no good reason. "Look at you, sitting around here all day, no job!" she'd say. "We can't support a freeloader like you for your entire life. Take a look around the village—everyone else has gone off to find work, then they come home at the end of the year brimming with pride and flush with cash. And yet you just sit there."

She had no idea how or where to go and find a job, but as it happened, her cousin was just about to set off to find work herself. She decided to tag along with her, and the two of them spent several days and nights on a bus, heading for Lhasa, a city she'd only ever heard of, and had certainly never set eyes on. That year, she had just turned seventeen. Turning up and landing a job in an unfamiliar city wasn't as easy as she had imagined. She spent days roaming the streets looking for work without any luck. Eventually, a friend of her cousin managed to set her up as an apprentice at a beauty parlour. As a trainee, she only got one hundred and fifty yuan a month, cash in hand, which was barely enough to keep her afloat, and she had to struggle through like this for some time. One day she received a call from her stepmother back in Sichuan: "It's been a year and you still haven't sent any money home! Did you go to Lhasa just to sunbathe?" Every time she called, the only words that came out of her mouth were about money. She could at least save on food since the beauty parlour provided some bare minimum fare, and the rent and all the bills were paid for by her cousin, who made more than she did at the restaurant where she worked. Of her pitiful monthly salary of one hundred and fifty yuan, she spent a hundred on the cheapest toiletries and necessities she could buy, then she scrimped and saved so she could send the remaining fifty back home to her family. She wore old clothes handed down from her cousin, and for hair ties she used elastic bands discarded by the customers at the beauty parlour.

She could never satisfy her stepmother's constant demands for money, so she decided that she had to find a better-paying job. One day, as she was mulling over what kind of work she could get, a couple of pretty, svelte women strolled into the beauty parlour and promptly spent close to ten thousand yuan on makeup and skincare products, casually taking handfuls of hundreds from their handbags and handing them to the owner. This was the first time she'd ever seen so much money, and it pained her when she compared it to the mere pennies she had in her pocket. She wanted to ask them how they made so much, but she didn't dare as she knew she'd get a scolding from the boss if she badgered the customers about something unrelated to business. However, she was soon able to tell what it was they did just from overhearing their conversations. At first, she felt disgusted by their money and looked down on them. And yet, she was toiling away at an honest job, and it had done nothing to help fill her purse, much less appease the demands of her hectoring stepmother. She spent several days thinking about how her own circumstances compared with those of the two women, and all of a sudden, she felt like she understood them now: the world isn't fair, it isn't easy to have a life with both money and self-respect, and they were just doing what they had to in order to get by.

The two women often came in to get facials. Every time they came, they were wearing something different—something pretty, something expensive—and their phones were always the latest ones on the market. Her view of them had now turned from disdain to envy. One day, while she was peeling a face mask off one of the women's soft, delicate skin, she asked the question as casually as she could: "Sister, it must be easy for you to make money where you are?"

"Yes, it is," said the woman proudly. "You can sit back, relax, and drink as much as you like, serve the customers, and you get fifty yuan a night. Open up your legs and give them special services and you'll be getting hundreds. There isn't a man alive who can resist the charms of a woman. A lot of men feel like life is dull without women like us, like food without salt." She seemed happy, at ease. "Your job must be pretty hard, but I bet if you put your nose to the grindstone, you can make a lot?" For a moment, Xiao Li didn't know how to answer. She glanced over at her boss, then held up five fingers to indicate five hundred. The girl responded with an offhand, derisive laugh. "Please! That wouldn't even pay for our skin cream! Come work at our place, you'll add a zero to your salary at the least. Doesn't matter what kind of work you do, it's all the same as long as there's money in it."

The other girl chipped in: "Sweetie, we're all pretty thick skinned where we work, and sometimes you have to pretend to be a little deaf. Anyway, pretty much no one talks about what you do for a living outside of there. When you go back home all people want to know is who brought back the most money. They don't care about what you've been through to get it, and they certainly don't care whether it's dirty or clean."

When she heard all this, her mind began to churn. Her boss had never had any worries about Xiao Li leaving before, but now that changed. Where would she find someone else to do all the odd jobs if she left? Only now did she suddenly realize she'd been paying her far too little all this time, and she kicked herself for not realizing it sooner.

The boss despised those two women from the bottom of her heart, but if they didn't come in for their facials, she'd be hundreds of yuan out of pocket, so she always welcomed them with a fake smile and gave them the best service possible. But it had never occurred to her that something like this might happen, that they'd put ideas in her employee's head. She wanted to say something to the girls, but she restrained herself. "You two ladies are blessed with natural good looks, and no man under the sun can resist a pretty woman and a good drink. But some girls have a false sense of their own beauty, like ugly ducklings pretending to be swans." The boss' implication fell on deaf ears, as Xiao Li now had her heart completely set on those red hundred-yuan bills. *Yes*, she thought, *fate is determined by heaven—what's the point in being coy about this? It's hard to stay afloat when you're away from home, and they're just doing what they need to do to make money. If I save up now while I'm young, I can buy myself some nice things when I go back home! Then I can get married to a man from a decent family and live a nice, honest life.* Not long after that, she began to gravitate toward the Rose.

People change over time. People's lives, and loves, are ever shifting, never permanent. But everyone has one goal that never changes: the pursuit of that word "happiness." Everyone has the right to pursue a happy life, and no matter what people do to pay the bills, it's always a happy life they're striving after.

2

Xiao Li stopped making a living with her labour and set out to make a living with her youth. Her income was twice what it was before, but her natural thriftiness didn't change in the least. She couldn't get along with the free-spending Chinese girls—she knew it was because of her frugality—and she continued to live a fettered life. It was at that point, when she had been left alone and friendless, that she was taken in by the kind-hearted Dahlia and Magnolia. But still, a leopard can't change its spots. Xiao Li liked to eat other people's food and avoid buying her own, and she liked even more to wear her sisters' clothes. One day, Dahlia remarked to Magnolia, "There's a lot of wildflowers where I'm from, and there's this one type of pink cassia that blooms the second the grass turns green, always getting there first before any of the others. We call it *tok lha*—'the hungry god.' This Chinese girl always seems to be hungry, doesn't she? I think that's the best name for her." From then on, Cassia had her new name, and the other Chinese hostesses at the Rose soon picked it up, too—to them she was *duo-la*, their Chinese pronunciation of *tok lha*. Azalea was the last of them to arrive, and Cassia accepted her immediately, thinking of her as another friend with a shared fate. Cassia was still as stingy as ever, but she was also humble and diligent. She was always cleaning up their little room of her own accord and even washing and folding the jumbled piles of clothes the girls left on their beds.

Cassia pinched every penny from her salary, and each month she sent half of it home and put the other half in the bank. Whenever she had free time, it was her habit to take her deposit book out of her handbag, examine it closely, smile to herself with satisfaction, then, ever so carefully, return it to the bag.

3

ONE NIGHT JUST LIKE ANY OTHER, THE OTHER THREE GIRLS came home, but dawn came and went with no sign of Cassia. She returned later that morning after it was already light and climbed into bed, breathing heavily through her sobs. When the others asked her what the matter was, Cassia said quietly, "Tibetan men are better when it comes to that stuff. If you make them happy, they sometimes get all soft on you and give you extra tips and things. But…" She continued to ramble on in this vein, testing the patience of the others, who were still half-asleep: "It's our down time and instead of going to bed you're crying and spouting silly nonsense. Get some sleep."

This caused Cassia to sob even harder. "Last night this old Chinese man took me to a hotel. I went with him quite happily at first, thinking I could make some more money. But I don't think he was right in the head—he knew I couldn't stand up to him and he spent the whole night grabbing me and smacking me around. But that was nothing. He gave me one thousand yuan to bite my breasts, and he almost bit my nipple off. Then he shoved a beer bottle into my vagina. I tried to fight him off but I couldn't. He said, 'Money can make people into demons, and it can make demons into people. I've paid for you, and you'll do what I want.' It just kept going and going." When she'd finished, she showed them her bloodied, mangled nipple and cried even harder than before.

The girls were dumbstruck. "The monster, the monster!" they kept saying, unable to come up with any other way to console her. After a moment, Magnolia suddenly spoke up, giving vent to her anger: "Thank the Three Jewels that he can't get his hands on every woman in the world. Even if he could, I bet he still wouldn't be satisfied. I hope the bastard dies, and soon."

Before all this, the girls had grown used to their work, and for a time they had been free from feelings of misery and powerlessness. But a string of terrible events had befallen them one after another: first there was what had happened to Azalea, then there was Dahlia's illness, and now tragedy had struck Cassia. All of this had left with them with the strong feeling that no matter how pretty their faces, no matter how nice the clothes they draped over their bodies, they would always have to suffer the scorn and abuse of others. They lamented their miserable karma, but their sorrow and their sense of aversion towards this life could do nothing to alter their fate. Though they felt repulsed by each and every one of the customers that came into the Rose, for the sake of their families and for their own survival, they flashed their white teeth and their counterfeit smiles, swayed their supple waists, and stuck out their chests and their asses to satisfy the men and get their money.

Six

1

DZOMKYI SET OUT, NO PLAN, NO DESTINATION, AND FEELING no attachment to her family. She carried nothing but an empty bag and the three thousand yuan she'd taken from home. She slowly made her way towards the bus station, wondering where exactly she should go. She'd been thinking about this carefully for several days now but hadn't come up with any ideas. There were several ticket windows at the bus station advertising a variety of local destinations, and she stood before them, torn between Chengdu and Lhasa. There was only half an hour until the buses departed, but she still couldn't decide where to go. There were always a lot of people heading from Chamdo to Chengdu, and she didn't want to run into anyone she knew. Better to go to Lhasa, at least that way she could turn the trip into a pilgrimage. Having made her spontaneous decision, she bought a ticket. When the time came to board, there was a throng of people seeing off their loved ones, reluctant to part, but Dzomkyi was all by herself. The bus set out, and just like that she was gone, feeling nothing at all for the place she was born and raised. All that was left for her there now was regret and sorrow.

Dzomkyi was sixteen years old, in the prime of her youth. She was tall and graceful with a head of soft, golden-tinged hair, so long it almost reached her heels. With every step she took down the street her braids swayed from side to side, and passers-by found their gaze helplessly drawn in her direction. If you took a good look at her face, you'd notice the straight nose, the big eyes like dawn stars, and the fair and delicate complexion. She was a beautiful young woman. And it was after her beauty had emerged in full force that the boys in her class had begun to kid around and flirt with her.

In her second year of high school, there was a boy from the year above who was constantly stopping her in the corridors outside class for no real reason, calling her name and giving her snacks or drinks. Eventually he just came out with it and told her he liked her. At first, she took no interest in the boy, in fact she found him annoying, but gradually she came to accept his ways, his dumb persistence. It's easy for a woman to develop a soft spot for a man who shows her affection, and in the end, the two of them fell in love. Before long, her thin frame began to flesh out, pimples broke out all over her previously delicate skin, and her belly started to swell by the day. Dzomkyi was sick with worry. She could hardly throw up what was in her belly, and she couldn't exactly get rid of it out the other end, either. Out of sheer desperation she tried to bind her stomach in using a scarf, but there was no holding back the signs of a growing life, and the size of her belly became more and more obvious. By the fourth month of pregnancy, she could feel the baby kicking, and she could no longer concentrate on her studies. She sought out the boy, who was madly in love with her, who'd said he wouldn't think twice about giving his life for her, and asked him what he thought they should do. "Don't try and scare me," he said indifferently. "Who knows if that child is mine or not? Besides, I have to get ready for the college entrance exams." He laughed lightly and strolled away without so much as a glance over his shoulder. From then on, he didn't call her name in the corridor anymore—in fact he avoided her like the plague. There was no one she could turn to—all her confidants had vanished like stars in the daytime—and she was left alone to figure out how to get rid of the child inside her.

When she was watching TV one day, she saw an ad for a clinic that sold abortion pills—cheap, painless, and guaranteed to work, they said. Dzomkyi memorized the address and went there the next morning to buy the medicine. She took the pills as soon as she got home, feeling happy and full of hope, then lay in bed with the covers pulled up over her head. After a while, she felt a prolonged, searing pain in her stomach that made her head spin, then she began to bleed profusely from her vagina, and finally she passed out. When Dzomkyi came to, she was in a hospital bed. She opened her eyes to see her mother, who immediately spat in her face, not in the least bit glad that her daughter had regained consciousness. "Disgraceful slut! You shouldn't have bothered waking up. How am I supposed to face people now?" When she was done, she walked out in tears. Dzomkyi didn't know what she felt more: fear or shame. She yanked the covers up over head so no one could see her and bit down hard on her lip. At that moment she wanted nothing more than to fly off into the sky, or for the earth to open and swallow her up.

Dzomkyi stayed in the hospital for a week, during which time her father, who wasn't much of a talker, brought her food every day, but her mother didn't come back once. Her father didn't comfort her, nor did he reproach her—the only thing he said was, "You have to eat well and recover your health." When her father's words broke the silence of the hospital ward, Dzomkyi closed her eyes, unable to even look at him, much less relate to him the torment she was feeling inside. She kept seeing her mother's fearsome expression and kept hearing those words over and over until it felt like her head was going to split open: "Disgraceful slut! You shouldn't have bothered waking up. How am I supposed to face people now?"

Her companions on the ward were a married couple from the country. The wife had been hospitalized after having a miscarriage and losing a lot of blood. From the look of it, they weren't very well off. The husband spent all his time vying to get a turn on the hospital's electric stove so he could make his wife some tsampa with tea and yak butter, which comprised her three meals a day, every day. He himself just drank plain tea. She never saw him put an ounce of butter in his cup, but when he put butter in his wife's tsampa, he always made it a generous lump. Sometimes the wife wrinkled up her nose, not wanting to eat. "You've got to try, dear," he'd say lovingly, "you need to keep up your strength." Very patiently, he would take a small amount of the tsampa and spoon it into her mouth. Even though she didn't want to eat, she didn't have the energy to keep putting up a fight, so she swallowed down the food like an obedient little girl, looking lovingly at her husband with dewy eyes.

From the rooms around them there came the sound of babies crying and the buzz of visitors chatting with patients, but except for the doctors making their rounds in the mornings and the odd visit from the nurse, no one else ever came to their ward, and it was exceptionally quiet. Sometimes the man dozed off and didn't notice his wife's IV bag was empty, so Dzomkyi called to him softly: "Uncle." The man would wake up, embarrassed, mumbling, "Oh, I drifted off again," then go to fetch the nurse. They didn't need their IVs in the afternoon and there wasn't anything to do in particular, so the man would sit and patiently pluck the lice from his wife's head as he intoned the *Praises to the Twenty-One Taras.* As her husband's hand touched her head, she either fell into a peaceful sleep and snored gently, or she lay still, gazing out the window, a look of happiness spreading across her face. Apart from his endless chanting, the man didn't say much else.

That old saying is true: "a happy home is scarce in samsara." This poor country couple was deeply in love, inseparable as a pair of swallows, but they hadn't been blessed with the child they so desperately wanted. Every day the husband did as the lama had instructed and recited the *Praises to the Twenty-One Taras*, he prostrated, made offerings, he did everything he could, but still she miscarried. When she got pregnant this time, they'd taken the advice of an elder and gone up to the stupa that overlooked their valley, where they performed countless circumambulations, calling each other "Mum" and "Dad" for good luck. But miscarriages seemed to have become a routine occurrence for them, and it had almost taken her life when it happened this time. Dzomkyi had overheard all of this when the nosy gossip of a nurse had been grilling the taciturn husband, dragging every possible detail out of him.

When the wife was sitting up in bed one day, her husband said gently, "I'm just twiddling my thumbs here. Why don't we make some use of this time? How about I finally get all the lice out of your hair!"

The wife laughed weakly. "Don't bother, it's too much trouble for you. Even if you manage it now, you won't have time to keep it up when we get home and they'll just come back. Why don't you come lie down with me instead?" She had him lie down on the bed, then took a bunch of keys from his waist on which there was a blunt pair of nail clippers, and she sat, carefully trimming his long, dirt-encrusted fingernails.

Dzomkyi peeked at them from her bed. *That woman has good fortune. She has a loving husband. Not like me with my wretched karma.* She cried bitter tears.

By the time she got out of hospital, she was emaciated and her eyes were sunken. Dzomkyi, who had always been boisterous and talkative, now became suddenly withdrawn. She stayed at home for a few months, then one day she picked up her backpack and went to school, determined to knuckle down and be a good student. Her mother had asked the school to grant her leave, telling them she was sick, but the funny way the teacher and the other students looked at her now made her feel deeply uneasy. Sometimes, in between classes, she'd catch the other kids whispering to each other, but as soon as they saw her coming they'd change the subject. Dzomkyi had no one she could confide in anymore, at home or at school. The worst thing of all was that strange way the teachers and the other kids looked at her, each sideways glance like an arrow striking her heart. It was torture, and she couldn't bear it. She didn't want to see those expressions anymore, and she didn't want to hear her mother's endless lectures. After one week, she ran away from home.

After several days and nights on the bus, she arrived in Lhasa. The anarchic, bustling city was completely unfamiliar to her, and she spent the first few days wandering the Barkhor and the alleys, staying at a cheap little guesthouse at night. When the money she had brought from home was almost all gone, she began to think about what she could do to support herself, and she hit the streets in search of work. Most of the wanted ads she came across were for restaurants looking for waitresses, a job she felt she wouldn't be any good at, so she ended up working at a clothes shop. It wasn't a big place, but it was in a great location and they did a brisk trade, a trade that increased even more with Dzomkyi's arrival. She spoke fluent Chinese and she was pretty, too, making her a hit with the young, flashy customers. At first the Chinese owner showered her with praise and gave her a raise at the end of the month, and she even had Dzomkyi eat her meals with her and her husband, who co-owned the store. She picked up pieces of meat with her chopsticks and put them in Dzomkyi's bowl, and only Dzomkyi was given her fancy treats. Getting this special care when she was away from home in an unfamiliar place brought some warmth to Dzomkyi's closed off heart and, for the first time in a long time, a smile reappeared on her lips. Her beautiful smile was a great attraction for the customers, but it also attracted someone else: her boss' husband. The husband, who was also Chinese, paid more attention to Dzomkyi than the other employees and he prized her more than the rest, constantly complimenting every aspect of her appearance and her job performance. One day when he was playing around, he grabbed her hand and started stroking it, right in front of the other employees.

"It's really beyond compare, Dzomkyi's hands are as soft and smooth as turquoise! You only have to look at them to know they're the hands of a princess. But you lot, you only need one glance at your hands to know they're the hands of servants."

Dzomkyi's face went bright red and she snatched her hand back. "Go to hell, you dirty old bastard!" she said in Tibetan, and the other girls broke into hysterical laughter. He didn't understand what she'd said, but he could tell she was cursing him, and he fled upstairs in embarrassment.

She'd been stung again, and it made her think back to the home and family she had left. But every time she did, she was reminded of that heartless, fickle boy and her mother's terrifying face. It was just salt in her wounds, and the thoughts of home naturally vanished. The best way to forget about the man's behaviour was to busy herself in her work, passing the days by throwing herself into her sales and her customer service. Since the business continued to prosper, the boss treated her even better than before: she let her wear any clothes from the store she liked and she was always sure to give her a bigger bonus than the others at the end of the month. But "the wind won't leave the prayer flags alone" and "the spirits won't let the raven rest"—in just the same way, as soon as the boss stepped out to take care of some business, that husband of hers with his little red pig eyes would come up with some excuse to call Dzomkyi upstairs.

Since that time Dzomkyi had pushed away his roaming hands and cursed him to his face, he hadn't dared to take such open liberties with her. One day he called her upstairs, and adopting an authoritative air, instructed her to come sit next to him and pour him a drink. Dzomkyi, oozing disdain, poured him an overflowing cup of water.

"If there's nothing else I'll be going back downstairs," she said coldly.

He jumped out of his chair in a fluster and seized her hand imploringly. "Be my mistress and I'll make sure you're taken care of!"

Right at that moment, the boss walked in. She took one glance at the scene before her, and without a single query, slapped Dzomkyi hard in the face.

"Filthy whore!" she spat in Chinese.

Without a second thought, Dzomkyi slapped her back even harder. "Take a look at your husband," she replied in Chinese. "If I ever considered being with someone like him, it'd mean that we Tibetans had run out of men! Count up what you owe me. I don't want to look at this disgusting creature for another second." The boss continued to curse her, foaming at the mouth with rage as she took out a handful of hundreds and threw them in Dzomkyi's face.

Dzomkyi picked up the money off the floor and put it in her bag, spat in the direction of her former employers, then walked out.

2

Dzomkyi went back to wandering the streets looking for a job, just like when she'd first arrived in the city, but nothing seemed like it would work out. She couldn't do physical labour—and she didn't want to, either. She thought again of the brightly lit classroom and deeply regretted not having cared for herself, not having valued herself. Yet she was surprised to find that it hadn't occurred to her at all to return home, to go back to her parents. *Maybe it's my fault for being naïve, or maybe it's Mum's fault for not seeing things my way. Either way, that old saying really does apply to me: "the child won't heed and the mother won't love."* She felt a shiver of cold deep inside.

She had made the decision not to return home, so she had to get a job to support herself, no matter what. Eventually she found something at a little café that served cold drinks. Though her wages weren't nearly as high as before, she got given two meals a day and she was very pleased with the job. By now she'd learned to speak the Lhasa dialect fluently. She smiled sweetly and spoke pleasantly as she greeted the customers, saying "Welcome," "Please have a seat," and "What would you like to drink?" just like a Lhasan would. The customers liked this very much, and some even said she was as beautiful as a goddess, which made her look at the floor in embarrassment and glance over at her boss, her face as red as an apple. When a customer complimented her appearance or her service, the jolly manager would come over and stroke her hair, then she'd say something like, "You should be happy, dear! Everyone likes a pretty girl. Even with cattle, everyone prefers the ones with the good coats, right?" Dzomkyi wouldn't say anything, but she'd feel happy and warm inside.

The café opened its doors around twelve noon. One day, right when they opened up, a young guy with dyed blonde hair and a thick gold chain came in and ordered a soda. Dzomkyi didn't pay much attention to him at first, but lunchtime rolled around and he was still sitting there, so Dzomkyi went over.

"Brother, would you like something else? It's lunchtime now, but we don't serve much food here I'm afraid, just drinks and snacks."

He stared at Dzomkyi with piercing eyes. "What? You still don't get it? As long as I can look at your face all day, I don't need any food."

She laughed lightly, trying to brush it off. "Brother, don't kid around. I'm not that much to look at. I'm no different from anyone else—two eyes, a nose, and a mouth."

"I've come across a lot of girls in my life, but you're the most beautiful," the boy replied seriously. "How about we get to know each other? Here's my number. You give me yours."

Dzomkyi took the piece of paper with his number on it. "I can't give you my number, I don't have a phone," she said. The boy was furious, thinking she was lying to him, and he stormed out of the place without a word.

He came back the next day, but it was later and the shop was already full of customers. He sat on a bench in the corner, hoping to get Dzomkyi's attention. When another waitress came up to take his order, he pointed at Dzomkyi and shouted, "I want that one!" When she heard the racket, Dzomkyi rushed over.

"What can I get for you?" she asked, patiently.

He pulled her over to his side and laid a hand on her shoulder. "You don't know it, but from the moment I laid eyes on you I haven't been able to eat or sleep. If you be my girlfriend, my sickness will be cured. I've got lots of money. You wouldn't have to be a waitress with me, you'd stay at home and live like a proper lady."

Dzomkyi was mortified and she pushed him away fiercely. "It's my karma to be a servant. I wouldn't know how to be a lady. Please don't come back here anymore."

When the other customers heard this exchange, some of them eyed Dzomkyi curiously, and some whispered amongst themselves about the young man's rudeness. At this point, the cheerful owner came over to defuse the situation with some tactful light-heartedness and flattery.

"Look lad, these are all simpleminded girls who've come in from the country. They can't be the kind of refined ladies you're after. Thanks to our protector Panden Lhamo, Lhasa is blessed with many beautiful girls. You can marry a city girl and live a happy life that'll be the envy of everyone!"

The boy didn't listen to a word she said. He got up to leave, but not before giving a parting shot: "Spare me all that, lady. Around these parts, I can get whatever I want. Haven't you heard of Wangchen from Liberty Gardens?"

Though she'd never laid eyes on this Wangchen from Liberty Gardens, according to what she'd heard, he was a local kingpin with a shady reputation. He liked to get in fights, and he won every time he fought. He always had a string of prayer beads wrapped around his wrist and he swaggered grandly down the street, a jacket draped over his shoulders and a long knife hanging at his waist. Sometimes, if businessmen were having problems calling in a debt, they'd hire him to go collect it for them. It was said that all he had to do was show up with a few of his goons, knock on the door, and the money would be handed over on the spot. If a man like that had taken a fancy to Dzomkyi, he was liable to do anything. Dzomkyi's short-lived peace of mind was once again thrown into disorder and she was left standing there blankly, unable to focus on the work before her.

"You're so lucky, Achak!" said one of her co-workers, enviously. "You've got looks, you've got a figure. We don't have your appeal—people don't even give us a second glance. They say the Buddha treats all beings in the six realms equally, but it doesn't seem very equal to me."

Dzomkyi sighed. "I'm like Nangsa Öbum, forced to marry the Prince of Rinang just because she had a pretty face. Everything that's happened to me is because of my looks. I wouldn't be in this mess otherwise. If I could give my looks away, I'd gladly give them all to you." Dzomkyi's co-worker shook her head in disbelief.

The next morning the phone rang at the café. The owner answered and called for Dzomkyi, saying it was for her. Dzomkyi looked at her boss sheepishly—employees weren't supposed to use the shop phone for personal calls. *Who could it be? I don't know anyone in Lhasa,* she thought. When she put the phone to her ear, she heard the voice of the blonde-haired boy, Wangchen, and she slammed the phone down in anger. The phone kept ringing every few minutes, blaring interminably, and in the end Dzomkyi picked up again. "There's no bad blood between us, why won't you just leave me alone? I'm going to go look for another job tomorrow. Please don't call here again." She hung up.

When Dzomkyi got back to her room that night, she felt empty and cold inside. She thought that no matter what she did, if she kept working at the café, that shameless man would never let her be and it would end up hurting the business. She considered it for a long time, and eventually she decided she had to give up her job at the café.

She told the owner the next morning. She was hugely disappointed, but she knew that Dzomkyi was right, and she let her go without putting up a fight.

"Ama," said Dzomkyi, welling up, "it's just like Nangsa Öbum said: my pretty face has become my own worst enemy. Ever since I came to Lhasa, I haven't been able to hold down a job, I've had to put up with gossip and slander, and it's just been one disaster after another—all because of my looks. I've given it a lot of thought and I know I have to leave, but I've got no idea where I'll go next, or what'll become of me."

"My dear," said the boss, stroking her hair, "you might have rotten karma, but it's not your fault you have a pretty face. What could be more of a blessing, being born into this world beautiful both outside and in? You're not just a pretty face. You're honest, you're reliable, you're capable. If the Three Jewels are watching over you, you'll have a happy life. Just don't forget about little old me, and remember to stay in touch, no matter what happens." Dzomkyi left, tears in her eyes, looking back over her shoulder again and again.

3

WHEN DZOMKYI ONCE AGAIN HIT THE NOW-FAMILIAR STREETS of Lhasa looking for work, it happened to coincide with the Rose's drive to hire new hostesses, and just like Dahlia, she signed up. Up until that point, Dzomkyi had walked a long, winding, and largely unlucky path when it came to finding work, so she felt that the Rose would be the best place for her. She accepted the job, completely indifferent to the contract ruse the boss had pulled on them. From then on, no one called her Dzomkyi anymore: she was Magnolia. Not only did she grow accustomed to the name, she started to like it; when people called her that, she felt happy, like she really was a brilliant magnolia flower. Now, the most valuable things she had left—in truth, the only things she had left—were what her mother had given her: a slender body like bamboo from Tsari, a pretty face, and an undisguisable youth, and she used this natural capital to support herself. Since Magnolia didn't have to give a thought to anyone else, she lavished her entire income on herself, enjoying it carefree. The other girls all assumed that her family must not want for money, and they envied her deeply.

Azalea even said this to her one day. "Achak, you're so different from us, having a well-off family. You'd be much better off going back to them instead of living this miserable life. At least you've got a place you can call home, a mother and a father."

Magnolia laughed derisively. "It's been three years since I left home. If my parents missed me, if they thought about me, they could come find me. Lhasa's big, but it's not that big." She lit a cigarette and exhaled a cloud of smoke, and with it a dejected sigh. Out of nowhere, a teardrop the size of a pea rolled down her cheek.

Though Magnolia had been to high school and therefore had more education than Azalea, she wasn't in the habit of reading anything apart from the missing persons ads in the evening papers, which she bought every day and kept in a cardboard box under her bed. One habit she did have was that she never missed an episode of her favourite radio show, "Melody Messenger."

Magnolia slowly wiped away her tears, then retrieved the stack of yellowed newspapers from under her bed. "Just look at how many missing persons ads there are in here. I've bought the evening paper every single day since I started working at the Rose. This box is stuffed with them, but where's my name? And "Melody Messenger" is always airing those notices: such-and-such a girl ran away from home and her parents have had no contact with her for however many years. Her family are extremely concerned about her and anyone with any information can contact them at such-and-such a number. Whenever I hear them, I always wish it were me. But I've been dead to my parents from the moment I brought shame on them." She burst into tears again.

Magnolia was a very tough person; she would never normally talk about such things and the others had never seen her cry before. She was always the queen of the club. From the outside she seemed carefree, content, happy, making her money at night and spending it lavishly during the day. Magnolia didn't just possess natural beauty, she had a sunny disposition that all the other girls lacked. No matter how many of the big clients at the Rose—both Tibetan and Chinese—professed their love and said they wanted her all to themselves, Magnolia liked keeping her freedom, liked having everyone call her "baby," and she never gave preferential treatment to any man in particular, only going along with whoever produced the most cash. She wouldn't fall for their smooth talk—in fact she didn't trust a single man under the sun, she thought they were all the same, heartless, fickler than a horse is fast or a sheep's tail is short.

And yet, despite Magnolia's total distrust of men, there had, at one time, been a Chinese client who she'd opened up to. She'd met with him several times and got to know him, and though he liked women and booze just like any other man, she thought this one had a good heart.

One time when he was drunk, he'd buried his head in her chest and poured out his troubles, crying tears of despair. "My wife is such a good woman. She's taken care of me all these years. And she's older than me, so I've never been bossy with her or made her suffer. We've been happily married more than twenty years now, but all this time I've been wanting a child. I've waited and I've hoped, but she's a chicken who can't lay an egg; her belly's never bulged like other women's. I've got lots of money now. How can a couple be without a child..."

His pitifulness stirred Magnolia's sympathies, but there wasn't much she could do to console him. "Don't be sad. It must be your karma," she said.

Her words gave him no comfort, in fact he became even more morose. "A man not having a child of his own means the end of his line. I'm my mother's only child, so the duty of carrying on the family line is on my shoulders alone." He seized Magnolia's hand, begging now. "You can change the way you live, you can bear me a child. If you can do that, I'll give you anything you want. You have to give me a child, please! You wouldn't just be my mistress anymore. We'll have a proper wedding and you'll be my wife. And if you really don't want to give up this life, I'll respect your decision, and I'll pay you for all your lost income during the pregnancy." The life he was describing was one that all the girls at the Rose dreamed of. When she heard this, Magnolia felt like the desires she'd cherished deep down inside for so long were finally being realized. *Finally, I'll have a partner I can find solace with and a home to call my own.* Rejoicing inside, Magnolia accepted his proposal.

She stopped using contraception when she was with him, and from then on, she only gave other customers the regular hostess services—her body belonged entirely to the Chinese man. But just like his wife, her belly refused to bulge.

The Chinese man grew anxious. He bought her all sorts of fertility drugs and nutritional supplements, and she began to visibly put on weight and her complexion became all blotchy, but still she couldn't lay the egg he wanted. He took Magnolia to get examined at all the major hospitals, and the consensus of the doctors was that her uterus was severely inflamed and that, for the time being at least, there was minimal chance of her conceiving.

One day he took Magnolia to a clinic, where he had a doctor he knew draw blood from her arm and run some tests. She didn't think there was anything unusual about this until she overheard the doctor in the next room going over STI treatments with his patient. She was no fool and she realized now that he hadn't brought her here to run any old tests, but to check for STIs.

Unlike other hospitals, the corridors in that place were eerily quiet. She sat alone on a bench, waiting for him. Although he hadn't said a word about it, she felt that he looked down on her, that he was mistreating her, and she felt a flame of anger burning within, so hot it was almost roasting her insides. He reappeared at that moment, grinning broadly and holding the sheet of paper with the test results. He was about to open his mouth when Magnolia snatched the paper from his hand. He looked at her in amazement, not sure what the problem was, and saw that her face had turned bright red and splotchy, her lips a deep scarlet. She looked at the paper in her trembling hands, but she couldn't read the English letters the doctor had written. She marched into the doctor's office and demanded an explanation of what was written on the paper.

"STI. It's the international acronym doctors use for sexually transmitted infections."

When she heard this, the flame of anger inside shot up, and unable to control it, she slapped the Chinese man hard in the face. "Animal. You've thought of everything, haven't you? All men are the same, all cut from the same cloth. You're all dogs. I've never seen a white crow in my life, only black ones." She turned and stormed out without looking back.

From then on, she knew that any man who promised to keep her as his mistress was delusional and simply indulging in his own fantasies. To anyone who made such offers, she said: "I don't know anything about being a mistress. The only thing I know is money." She went back to the way she was before: not favouring any man, just going along with whoever produced the most cash.

It was a summer morning, and when the other girls woke up at their usual time, Magnolia made a sudden announcement out of the blue: "I've dreamt a lot about my mother recently, the old tigress. Lhasa has changed so much in the last few years, but I have no idea what's changed back home, and I have no idea how my parents are doing now." This was the first time she'd expressed such feelings about her parents and her home.

Azalea looked at her, a little enviously. "Achak, if I were you, I'd go back home. Even with a bleeding heart we have to go out there and serve the men, smiling our smiles and flashing our teeth. See, I still can't get used to the terrible smell of their breath: the garlic, the booze, the cigarettes. I feel like no matter where I am, I can still smell it, and it smells like shit. Just thinking about it makes me feel sick." The others all knew exactly what she meant. None of them said anything, but at that moment they all felt a sudden wave of revulsion.

On the surface, Magnolia had always given the impression that she had no attachment whatsoever to her home and her parents, but now it was finally clear that she had wilfully locked all those feelings away and had never let go of them deep down inside. The room fell quiet. After a while, Cassia retrieved her deposit book from underneath her pillow and started looking through it eagerly, as she always did. She counted to herself on her fingers—one, ten, a hundred, a thousand, ten thousand—and a look of satisfaction came over her face.

"Look, on top of all the money I've sent home, I've got exactly fifty thousand in my account! Tomorrow I'm going to go to the bank and get myself a card. I think it's time I went back home. I can use all the money I've saved up to open a little business in town."

"Yes," said Dahlia, "I think it'd best for all of us if we went back home. But I…" She felt a tingle in her nose and couldn't go on.

The four women lived their lives in that little room, sharing all their joys and sorrows. Even though it wasn't big, it was a place of their own, somewhere they could come back to. But no matter how much comfort the little room gave them, it would never be anything more than a temporary shelter from the wind and the rain; it wasn't a true home, a place they were attached to, a spiritual sanctuary. They couldn't stay there forever. The girls resolved a lot of their inner conflicts that day, and in the end, it was decided that Dahlia would check in to the hospital and that Magnolia and Cassia would return home. Azalea withdrew all of her savings and went with the other three to the hospital to help take care of the formalities, after which she planned to stay and look after Dahlia.

Before leaving the hospital, Cassia took five hundred yuan from her purse and gave it to Dahlia. This decision had required a steely determination on her part, but even still she was loath to part with the money, and she caressed the bills for a good while before handing them over.

"Achak, when I was all alone, you took me in and looked after me. I'm grateful to you from the bottom of my heart. But we're all powerless, so…" She trailed off awkwardly before picking up elsewhere. "It's not much, but it's my way of showing my thanks. Make sure you call me and keep in touch. You're a good woman, and with the blessing of the Buddha, I'm sure you'll get better."

Magnolia didn't have any money to give—even her bus ticket had been bought for her by Azalea. She thought for a moment, then with no hesitation, removed her gold necklace and her gold ring and handed them to Azalea.

"Dahlia," she said, "I don't have any money to give you. I've got used to living a lavish life; even that bail money was paid for by little sister Azalea—I hadn't forgotten. I'm giving this jewellery to her. If you're hard up, sell it. When you've got money, it's jewellery; when you haven't, it's food and clothes. Don't forget to call me." She threw her arms around Dahlia, tears in her eyes.

Dahlia had so much she wanted to say to her sisters, but she couldn't find the words, and it all remained unsaid. She hugged Magnolia and Cassia. "We come from different places, we're even different races, but our karma has bound us together. Now we're going our separate ways all of a sudden, and I feel..." Dahlia couldn't go on.

Azalea couldn't bear to drag out the separation any longer. "Achak Drölkar, it's time for them to go now. It's no good for someone to set off on a journey crying. I'm going to go see them off at the bus station." The girls left the hospital, looking back at Dahlia, reluctant to part.

The bus was about to leave, but they simply stood there, holding one another tightly. Seeing how hard it was for them to part ways, the driver sympathized, but he had a schedule to keep to, and he gave them a light tap of the horn to signal that it was time to leave. The girls finally let go and Magnolia and Cassia boarded the bus, their eyes filled with tears. As the bus pulled out, Azalea ran alongside waving them off, and the three of them called out to each other through the windows.

Two of Azalea's beloved sisters had left for home. In that moment, she too couldn't help but feel that she wanted to go back to her own home. The bus was gone. Even the dust stirred up by its tires had settled. She felt cold and empty inside.

Azalea had nothing in particular to do on the first day that Dahlia was in hospital. Her initial plan after seeing off her sisters had been to go to the Jokhang Temple and pray before the Jowo, but she changed her mind when she saw how many pilgrims there were. She had an aversion to crowds now—the emptier and quieter the place, the better. After leaving the bus station, Azalea headed straight to Sera to pray to Hayagriva, the protector deity of the monastery. Outside the monastery gates she bought three butter lamps and a *khata* scarf for offering, then went inside to pray for Dahlia's speedy recovery. As she had hoped, there were fewer pilgrims than usual at Sera that day, and she was able to take her time before the statue of Hayagriva. She circumambulated the shrine once for every year of Dahlia's life, praying for her with all her heart. Having accomplished her goal, she felt comforted. *With the love and compassion of the Three Jewels, my Achak will get better*, she thought, and a sense of peace came over both her mind and body. By the time she had finished all her prayers it was past noon. There were even fewer pilgrims around than before, and the monastery's shrines, streets, and circumambulation paths had all fallen quiet. She had found that elusive tranquil space.

Her steps took her towards the Lingkhor. She treaded lightly up the stone stairway, listening to the birdsong emanating from the willow groves that flanked the path and the sound of the waterfall tumbling over the high cliffs. She hadn't felt this happy in years. She hadn't heard the sounds of wild birds and a cascading waterfall since the age of thirteen, the time she'd first arrived in the city. It was a completely different world from the dark, confined surroundings of the Rose. Every blade of grass and drop of water was pure, clean, and unspoiled; the birds were so free and at ease. There were no bright lights on the Lingkhor and there was no ear-splitting music. The birdsong was even more beautiful than the music of the Gandharvas, and the elegant trees and the rushing waterfall would put paradise to shame. As Azalea walked up the spotless steps, enjoying the splendour of nature, she came across an old bag by the side of the stairs that contained some loose change, and she placed one yuan inside as she always did when giving alms to beggars. After she'd proceeded a little further, she saw an old woman who looked like a nun; she was wearing a big black apron, a headscarf, and a mask, and was chanting *manis* as she swept each of the steps. As Azalea walked past, not paying her much mind, the woman stopped her sweeping and said, "Be careful dear, the steps are steep," then bent her head and returned to her work. The voice of the woman in the nun's clothes seemed so familiar, and somewhere in the back of her mind it stirred a memory of someone from back home who she'd known when she was young: Butri. The last time Azalea had seen her was the year Butri had come back to their village in search of waitresses for her restaurant. She was swarthy and fat as a pig back then. The woman in the nun's clothes standing before her didn't look at all like Butri, but she sounded exactly the same, and when Azalea inspected the woman closely, she knew it was her. Butri, once as fat as a pig, was now thin and hunchbacked. Though her face was covered, the traces of the years were clear in the wrinkles at the corners of her eyes. Her formerly swarthy complexion had turned white and delicate, as though the melody of the *manis* had washed away the sins and cleansed her, body and mind.

Azalea recalled what Dahlia, in floods of tears, had told her about the terrible events of that freezing winter night. Azalea had been consumed with fury at the appalling things Butri had done, and presently she thought about how the person responsible for the horrible, heartbreaking circumstances Achak Drölkar now faced was none other than the woman standing before her in the handsome dress of a nun. Everything in front of her went black. If she'd run into Butri before, Azalea might have spat right in her face, but coming across her in a place like this threw her off guard. That was understandable—today, out of the blue, she'd been reminded of things she never wanted to be reminded of, and she'd run into someone she never wanted to run into. Her heart pounded and her body trembled, but Azalea said nothing and tried to calm herself down. The woman before her had no idea of the turmoil she felt inside. The woman in nun's clothes had gone back to her daily, unchanging task, sweeping the stairs with the broom she held in one hand, and muttering *manis* as she plied a string of prayer beads in the other.

Azalea stared at the nun. *Is she repenting for her past actions? Or is she praying to be reborn in the Pure Realm?* As she thought about this, the fire of anger burned inside her again. At that moment, the woman, as though she knew what Azalea was thinking, suddenly raised her voice and chanted louder. The melody of the *manis* was so pretty and touched her so deeply that it gradually cooled her wrath. Azalea took a fifty yuan note from her purse and put it in the collection bag, a move that surprised even herself. *Why am I giving her money? I'm in desperate need of it right now. What if one day I, too...* she didn't dare finish the thought. Shaking her head briskly, she hurried away.

Seven

1

DAHLIA'S HOSPITAL WARD WAS A FAR CRY FROM THEIR LITTLE rented room. Everywhere you looked, everything was white. On the first day she arrived, it had all felt so strange and unfamiliar. The girls' rented room was a little city apartment, a dim place with small windows and a small door. In fact, the doorframe was so low that they'd bang their heads when they came in if they weren't careful. The ward she was staying on now had huge windows, which gave her a feeling of complete emptiness. On her second day in the hospital, she had to have a battery of tests done on her lungs, heart, and liver. These tests alone used up much of the money she'd already put down for the deposit, and they were just standard hospital procedures that weren't even specifically related to her condition. The gratuitous expense tormented Dahlia deeply.

For the next week after the tests the doctors didn't tell her anything, they just gave her IVs to ease the inflammation. On the Monday of the second week the results came in. She had an advanced case of syphilis that was now beyond straightforward treatment. The best thing to do, they said, was to operate and cut out the decayed flesh. This was just the official declaration of her illness; it wasn't as though she was suddenly finding out about it for the first time, and it caused her no greater anguish than before. She knew by now that it was rotten down there. The stench of decay grew worse by the day, and she recognized that surgery was the best thing to do. She had an additional source of anxiety now: she had to find a surgeon who'd be willing to perform the operation as soon as possible, but how could someone of her lowly status possibly have connections like that? Who could she turn to for help? Azalea was no less worried than Dahlia. The two of them were beside themselves trying to figure out what to do, and it was then that the doctor who had originally diagnosed Dahlia, whose name they still didn't even know, came to see her.

"Don't worry, you two," the doctor said, approaching Dahlia's bedside. "I've already arranged with a surgeon I know to perform the operation as soon as we possibly can. Whatever you end up doing with your life, I think it's best if you give up this sort of work. All actions have consequences." The doctor's words made them both feel ashamed, and they looked at the floor, not knowing what to say. "You need to keep your strength up and get lots of rest before the operation," the doctor said, softening her tone. Just as she was about to go, Dahlia, tears of gratitude in her eyes, reached out her bony fingers and seized the doctor's soft, white hand. All she could say was "Thank you, thank you," over and over again. The doctor looked at Dahlia and smiled gently, as if to say that it wasn't necessary, then left the room. Azalea followed her out, telling the doctor she must have been sent from heaven and offering her own profuse gratitude.

Thanks to the doctor, Dahlia's surgery was scheduled sooner than they had thought possible. Around eight o'clock on the night before the operation, Azalea was called to the doctor's office to go through the various pre-op arrangements. The doctor said a lot of things about the procedure, the most alarming of which was "If the surgery isn't successful…" When she heard this, Azalea felt like they had come to the hospital and paid all these medical bills just so Dahlia could die here, and she even thought about calling the whole thing off. The doctor seemed to know what she was thinking. "Before an operation, doctors always go over worst-case scenarios and don't say much about the positives. It's just part of our job. The point of the surgery is to treat the illness, and right now the chances of success are over ninety percent." The doctor spoke with complete self-assurance, and it gave Azalea some small measure of comfort. It was Azalea's greatest wish that Dahlia would beat this sickness, and with trembling hands she signed her name in Chinese on the operation consent form. On the white sheet of paper, the two Chinese characters for "Yangdzom" were written in black ink.

When they signed their names at the Rose, the other girls all used their nicknames—Azalea was the only one who signed with her real name. She felt that the only things left in the world that belonged to her were what her parents had given her: her body and her name. She hadn't been able to look after her body, but no matter what happened, she would hang on to her name. Whenever she put pen to paper to write the two syllables "Yangdzom," her penmanship was always perfect.

2

DAHLIA WAS TAKEN INTO SURGERY THE NEXT DAY. AS SHE WAS being wheeled into the operating theatre, she clasped Azalea's hand, staring at her intently with her sunken eyes.

"If I don't make it out of here, you must keep my illness a secret.

Especially from the people back home—my family, our friends. They can never know."

Though Azalea was terrified, she didn't let it show. "Don't say such ominous things, Achak Drölkar. I'll wait for you in the corridor. You're the only family I have left in the world—where are you planning on going, leaving me all alone? Once you're all better we'll go back to our old home together." Azalea sat on the bench outside the door of the operating room, waiting. Her mind was on fire and her insides churned. She pressed her hands together tightly, praying that everything would be okay.

It wasn't long before Dahlia was brought out of the operating theatre. When she heard the doctor say, "The operation was a success," Azalea was delirious with joy; clasping her hands together, she said, "Just and merciful Three Jewels, thank you for bringing my Achak back safely!" She thanked the doctor repeatedly. As the nurse was attaching Dahlia's IV, she spoke to Azalea, irritably. "The patient will have to be on oxygen for a while as she's still in a weak state, and she'll need to be hooked up to monitors twenty-four hours a day. The deposit you put down before has all been used up, so you'll need to pay immediately." She handed Azalea a prescription with a long list of medicines written on it. "And listen, she's going to need special care, so be sure to put more in the account this time."

Azalea took the bank card containing all her savings and went to pay the medical bills. She presented the prescription the nurse had given her at the payment window, and from behind it there emanated a series of beeps as the clerk deftly tapped the numbers into her calculator. Now she finally understood why people always said that "the damn hospital calculator never subtracts, it only adds." The woman at the payment window sat there indifferently, blowing bubbles with her chewing gum. "You owe three thousand on top of the deposit you put down," she barked. Her jarring tone brought Azalea to her senses and she passed her card through the slot in the window. There was only about five thousand left in her account now and she was worried about how long it would last. In the midst of fretting about the medical bills, she suddenly remembered the jewellery that Magnolia had given her before she left, and she felt slightly better.

As Azalea returned to the corridor, preoccupied with thoughts of those fees racking up one after the other, an older woman was coming slowly toward her from the opposite direction. As they passed one another, the woman looked at Azalea in amazement, but Azalea's mind was only on the medical bills and she continued on her way, eyes fixed straight ahead, paying no attention to her. The woman stopped and made a strange noise to herself as she turned back to glance at Azalea, then she came around in front and looked at her full in the face.

"Girl, it's you… I'm not mistaken. It's really you," she said.

Azalea hadn't even registered the woman's presence before, but now that she was paying attention, she realized the woman standing before her was the last person in the world she wanted to see: Ms. Drölma. Everything went black before her eyes and a fire of anger rose inside, working itself into a fuming hatred. At the same time, an image of Mr. Nyendrak's kindly face nudged its way into her mind. With his gentle words echoing in her ears, she felt all her worldly hostilities ebbing away and the fire of wrath inside her calmed.

Still, she was hardly pleased. *Why the hell do I keep running into these people I don't want to see?* She tried not to let her emotions show and pulled back her lips in the pretence of a smile.

"Achak, I think you've got the wrong person. I don't know you."

She was about to leave when Drölma said, "Girl, my memory's not what it used to be and sometimes I can't tell my right from my left, but I'd recognize you anywhere. Yangdzom, I've done such terrible things to you in this life." She seized Azalea's hand tightly and a sombre look of remorse came across her wrinkled face.

The sudden sound of that horrible voice ringing in her ears brought up memories that Azalea had never wanted to be reminded of. Her insides churned and that intense fire of anger flared up again, binding her body and mind with an unbearable pain as though the fire was about to consume her entirely. It took every ounce of her self-restraint to calm it again.

She spoke coolly, not wanting to do or say a thing to convey her true feelings. "Achak, you've definitely got the wrong person. I don't know anyone called Yangdzom. I'm afraid you've –" She was desperately trying to restrain her feelings as she spoke, but she could hear her voice beginning to waver. Ms. Drölma didn't wait for her to finish, and spoke more forcefully now.

"Girl, please don't talk like that. I know you don't want to see me, and I don't blame you. But Yangdzom, ever since you left our house, Nyendrak and I have never given up looking for you and Tenzin Lhadzé, but we never heard a thing about either of you. Where have you been all these years?" She shook Azalea by the shoulders, but Azalea stayed silent and offered no response, leaving Drölma dumbfounded. "You have to believe me, girl, we looked for you all over Lhasa. Nyendrak, especially, still blames himself. He's always saying that he owes you so much. I'm telling you the truth—when it all became clear to me, what happened back then, I felt nothing but shame." She fell silent for a moment, then went on. "Where are you living now? What are you doing for work? It looks like you're doing well for yourself!"

Azalea just smiled. "Achak, that innocent little country girl that you knew is long gone. What's the point in asking all this now? It hasn't got the slightest thing to do with an arrogant, self-absorbed woman like you. We're making a living and getting by in the country, then people like you come along and whisk us off to the city with all your slick talk. For years you made me do the lowliest work, fed me the cheapest scraps, picking fault with everything I did, and as if that wasn't bad enough, you go and accuse me of stealing. I had no choice but to run away. I couldn't go home and I didn't know how to get by in the city, so I ended up going down the wrong path, and that's the fate of all us country girls here. People like us will never be able to escape the clutches of city people, or people with money. And don't tell Mr. Nyendrak that you saw me. I'm not that Yangdzom anymore. He's a good man, and with the blessing of the Three Jewels, he'll find happiness."

Ms. Drölma shook her head sadly, then she launched into a breathless speech. "Ever since you and Lhadzé left home, we've had no news about either of you. My daughter vanished off the face of the earth, just like you did. Nyendrak and I searched Lhasa from top to bottom but couldn't find her. At first we heard that she was working as a waitress at a teahouse in Lhodrak, but when we went there we didn't find her. Someone else said they'd seen a girl at a bar nearby who might be her, but she wasn't there either. Later on, we were told people had spotted someone who looked like Lhadzé in Chengdu, so the two of us went and we stayed there for a whole year searching for her, but still nothing. Some people said she'd been trafficked to China and sold to a Chinese man as a bride. Some said she'd fled to India. But we never found out anything for sure—she could have vanished into the sky or been swallowed up by the earth for all we know. The whole thing caused Nyendrak to fall sick with worry, and he hasn't recovered since. He doesn't go out during the day, he can't sleep at night, and his health has just got worse and worse. He takes the medicine I get for him, but he absolutely refuses to see the inside of a hospital. My health is getting worse, too, and I desperately need a maid to help out at home, but it's hard to find a good girl like you nowadays. There's a doctor I know who gives Nyendrak the medicine he needs. That's why I'm here now."

Hearing this made Azalea picture Nyendrak again, his tender expression. She felt deeply sorry for him. In that moment she wanted to offer some consolation to Drölma, and she was on the verge of saying something, but those words were swallowed back down when she thought about everything that had happened to her, and the fact that the person responsible for all her torment was the very woman standing in front of her. Then again, she also considered everything that had happened to be her karma, which was how she comforted herself, and the ageing woman standing before her today was certainly deserving of compassion. Her face was wrinkled, her back was bent, her hair was greying and dishevelled—it was clear that Ms. Drölma, formerly vain and elegant, had undergone many hardships. Once again, the hatred she felt towards this woman abated, and she felt sorry for her.

"Life is hard to predict, Achak. None of us knows when we'll have to part this world, so there's nothing more important than treasuring what we have and who we have while we're still here. You've only got Mr. Nyendrak with you now, so take good care of him and don't give him a hard time. And please don't tell him you spoke to me. It's best if he doesn't know I'm still in the city. He's a good man." As she spoke, she wiped away the tears that at some point had begun splashing onto her cheeks.

Ms. Drölma, too, was tearing up. For Drölma, once so full of herself, crying had become an everyday occurrence. "No matter what you say," she said, wiping her eyes, "we lived together for a time, and you should come back to us. It's the same place as before. I was suspicious and proud back then and it was all my fault, not yours. Our family owes you a lot. Now I'm old and my only daughter has vanished without a trace. My karma has come around."

"I've never blamed anyone, Achak. Whatever happens to me, good or bad, it's all determined by my actions in a previous life." Azalea ended the conversation there, then turned around and walked resolutely away. Ms. Drölma didn't go after Azalea even though she wanted to, perhaps out of shame, or a knowledge that she'd never catch up. She had no choice but to go her own way, every now and then casting a glance back over her shoulder.

3

IT HAD BEEN A WEEK SINCE THE OPERATION, BUT DAHLIA STILL hadn't recovered—in fact her condition had worsened. She was running a high fever, her sores still hadn't gone away, and the scar from the surgery had turned a dark purple. Even more worryingly, her thigh had also turned a dark purple. A few days later, lesions broke out elsewhere on her body, lesions that wouldn't stop bleeding and oozing pus. When Azalea saw this she became restless with terror, but with no way to help, she just wept and sighed in anguish. The one thing she *could* do was to be a good nurse for Dahlia, so she shuttled back and forth from the hospital cafeteria, bringing her noodles and vegetable dishes. Not wanting to disappoint her, Dahlia forced herself to eat a couple of mouthfuls, but she'd completely lost her appetite now and she couldn't manage any more than that. Azalea persisted and kept trying to make her eat, but Dahlia shook her head and screwed up her mouth, refusing to have another bite. Azalea had no choice but to take the rest and eat it herself.

Dahlia continued to show no sign of recovery, and a week later they received another bill. The nurse issued them a warning: "Her condition is serious and we're going to need to try some new medicines, expensive ones. If you don't pay on time her treatment will be stopped." This was said without an ounce of sympathy; on the contrary, she spoke assertively and grandiloquently, as though she were making a heroic announcement. But no matter what medicine they used, it was obvious that Dahlia's condition was deteriorating. She ran a fever day and night, and sometimes she became delusional, saying things like, "Open the door! Mum and Dad are here. And my brother, too."

The attending doctor took Azalea to one side and told her that Dahlia's condition was extremely grave, that there wasn't much hope, and that she should start preparing for the worst. Azalea had braced herself to hear something like this from the moment Dahlia's condition had begun to regress, but now the doctor was suddenly saying it for real it seemed like a bolt out of the blue. She felt dizzy, there was a ringing in her ears, and her heart flooded with pain. Kneeling before the doctor, she begged him. "Doctor, please do whatever you can to save my Achak. I'll figure out the money. She's the only person I have left in the world." The doctor shook his head, indicating that there was nothing they could do. She knew now that her precious sister would be taken from her, and she thumped her head against the wall, trying to stop herself from crying out. The doctor said some perfunctory words of consolation and then went off to see his other patients. Azalea sat in the doctor's office alone for a long time, crying. Eventually she wiped her face clean, fixed her hair, and walked out of the office as though nothing had happened. Suppressing her emotions, she gently opened the door to Dahlia's room and approached her bed, forcing a smile.

"Achak, the doctor just called me to his office, he said the reason you've been feeling worse is because the medicine is starting to take effect. That means you should be getting better soon!" As she said this, her face was flushed, she felt a searing pain inside, and she wanted to scream.

Dahlia didn't seem to notice her unusual manner, but still she took Azalea's hand and said, "Yangdzom, I know exactly what the situation is. There's no hope for treating it, so stop spending your money. Even if you were a bank you couldn't get your hands on the amount they're asking for. I can't set my mind at ease, knowing that I'm going to another place, but you still have to stay here. You can barely take a step in the city without money. I want to get out of here and go back home, back to where I belong."

"Achak, you should relax and focus on getting better," said Azalea, wiping away her tears. "You don't need to worry about the bills. One of your old clients heard about what happened and said he'd pay for everything. I'm going to get the money from him in a bit. You just wait for me."

Dahlia strained to focus on her as she left the room. "Silly girl," she said to herself. "Still dreaming her happy daydreams, even now." She closed her slender eyes and a trickle of tears rolled softly onto the pillow.

4

Azalea exited the hospital and found herself on the bustling streets, but she had no idea where she should go. She sat under the shade of a willow tree by the side of the road. She wasn't quite sure when it had happened, but spring had arrived and the festival of Saga Dawa was upon them. Pilgrims packed the City of the Gods every year at Saga Dawa; they circled the Lingkhor day and night, performing what virtuous deeds they could and celebrating the birth, enlightenment, and passage into nirvana of the Buddha. Some went to buy fish from the Chinese shopkeepers and set them free in the river, some went to get change at the bank so they could give alms to the poor. In the past, Azalea and her sisters would have been with them, wearing their face masks and making their rounds of the Lingkhor on the auspicious days of the 8th, 15th, and 30th, giving whatever alms it was in their power to give. Even the penny-pinching Cassia came with them and handed out money to the beggars. But now the sisters had all separated, and it wasn't even certain if Dahlia would live. Azalea was inconsolable. *If I had a beggar's skills, I'd do what they do—put Achak Drölkar in a cart and wheel her around begging for money for the medical bills. Maybe I'd even make a few thousand in a day. But I wouldn't dare. What should I do? I already told her I was going to get money from one of her clients. What client? All those men who used to buzz around us like flies, where are they now? Who can the helpless turn to for help?* She sat there in tears, completely despondent. The people around her were engaged in conversations or plying their prayer beads and spinning their prayer wheels. Not a single one of them paid her any mind. She took the necklace and the ring that Magnolia had given her from their cloth wrappings and looked at them closely. She decided to sell the necklace and keep the ring to remember her sisters by. Sliding the ring onto her finger and wrapping the necklace back up in the cloth, she headed to the Tromsikhang, where there were Khampa merchants who dealt in jewellery.

The market had been a trading spot for turquoise, coral, and *dzi* beads since ancient times. The ostentatious Khampa traders sported strings of coral and *dzi* around their necks and bore fistfuls of precious stones. The Khampas wore *chubas* with the right sleeve left hanging loose; they huddled together then haggled via secret finger signs exchanged inside their sleeves, and once the price was settled on, they went elsewhere to close the deal—cash rarely changed hands on the spot. The majority of these Khampa traders were men; there were hardly any women. The few that you did see were also draped in so much turquoise and coral that it looked like their necks had shrunk.

Azalea stood for some time watching the Khampa men haggling, clutching the gold necklace in her hand, not daring to take it out. A young guy wearing Chinese clothes kept eyeing her, and after a while she approached him.

"Excuse me, do you buy gold necklaces here? I need cash in hand, so I'm willing to sell it cheap," she said, getting straight to the point.

The young Khampa man grabbed her hand. "*Ah tsi*, I don't buy gold, gorgeous, but I'd like to buy you. How much?"

She pulled away from him forcefully. "Let go of me, you punk!"

The lad laughed dismissively and shoved her. "I've seen plenty of your type, selling fake gold. Don't come around here, giving the place a bad name. Why don't you piss off." He raised his hand as though to hit her. Azalea was furious, but she realized that this was no place for her, and she walked out in a hurry. She went to the Barkhor, where she singled out the wealthy, stylish women making their way round the loop, then approached them furtively and flashed the necklace.

"Achak, look at this lovely necklace. I need the money so I'm selling it."

Several people took a look, some even made an offer, but the amount was never anywhere near what she needed. One woman bit the necklace and said, "You say it's real, but these days it's easy to mistake brass for gold. Will you take a hundred?" Azalea shook her head, looking dispirited. The woman said, "How about one fifty. I can't go any higher." When Azalea shook her head again, the woman simply walked off without looking back. "When you've got money, it's jewellery; when you haven't, it's food and clothes"—that's what Magnolia had said when she'd given her the necklace, but now it seemed like nothing more than a piece of scrap metal. Azalea was dragging herself around the Barkhor, completely shorn of hope, when out of nowhere someone came up from behind and put their hands over her eyes.

"Do you know who I am?" said the woman in Chinese. She didn't let go until Azalea shook her head in response. When Azalea turned to see who it was, she didn't show the least bit of surprise.

"What? Have you seen enough? Yeah, that's right. I'm flat broke."

"You're such strange ones, you lot," said the Chinese woman, looking surprised. "When you left, you all left together. The clients were always asking for you four by name. You earned a lot, the work was easy—what's the sense in packing that in to come and wander the streets? This is no kind of life. The door of the Rose will always be open to you and the other girls." Despite the woman's eagerness, Azalea said nothing, as though she hadn't even heard her. After a moment, she took out the necklace and showed it to her.

"I know you recognize this. You've got money, and you like to wear gold. Buy it from me. I need the money."

The Chinese woman took the necklace in her hand and looked at it with amazement. "*Ai ya*, isn't this Magnolia's? How come you've got it?" Her eyes were glued to the necklace.

Azalea sized up her former boss' astonished expression. "That's none of your business. I didn't steal it, if that's what you're thinking. It's up to you if you want to buy it or not. You know that this cost eight thousand originally. Magnolia is fickle with her jewellery and she decided to pass it on to me. I'll take four thousand for it, and not a penny less." She spoke bluntly and decisively, giving the impression that she, too, was a woman of status and means.

Her ex-boss took the money from her handbag without a moment's hesitation. As she handed it to Azalea, she said, "We might not be close, but we've had some times together. Whatever your troubles, you can always come back to the Rose. At least there you won't go hungry and you won't want for money. When you spend your cash, people only care about the money, they don't care where it came from or if it's clean." Her appeal for Azalea to return to the Rose fell on deaf ears, as by the time she'd finish speaking, Azalea was already walking off into the distance.

Azalea went straight back to the hospital and pushed the cash through the slot in the payment window. "Sir, please hurry. She needs her IV."

The man behind the counter responded with a contemptuous and unfeeling rebuke. "So you've just left her by herself this whole time?"

Azalea didn't answer him. She ran straight to Dahlia's ward, wiping the sweat off her brow.

Dahlia was running a high fever and had passed out. When the other patient in the room saw Azalea come in, she cast her a disapproving look. "Unbelievable! Her condition is this bad and you're nowhere to be found! They decreased her dosage today because the bills hadn't been paid. She's been raving this whole time because of the fever." She continued to mutter some other complaints under her breath. Ignoring the other patient, Azalea clutched Dahlia's hand and called her name. Dahlia opened her eyes a crack and stroked Azalea's cheek with a thin, leathery hand. "I've caused you so much trouble," she said. It took all of her concentration to get those few words out, and when she'd said them, she closed her eyes again. Now that Azalea had put down more money, the nurse came in and reattached Dahlia's IV. Dahlia had become confused again. "Yangdzom, open the door! My mum and dad and brother are here to see me. And your mum and dad are here, too." She was delirious, and Azalea couldn't bear to see her in this state. She went to the doctor's office to get an update on Dahlia's condition.

"It's good that you've come," the doctor said when she entered. "If you hadn't, I was planning to go find you. The outlook is not good. She's been running a fever for several days now, the inflammation has spread to her eyes, ears, and brain, and we haven't been able to reduce it. If this continues and the fever doesn't subside, I'm afraid the only thing to do is to contact her family and prepare for the end. She's so young, and I can't bear to see this happen either, but her condition is grave and there's nothing we can do." There was genuine sadness in his voice.

Azalea had done everything in her power to get Dahlia better, and this was the result. She stood alone in the corridor crying, which was the only thing she could do at this point. After some time, she took out her phone and called Magnolia in Chamdo. From the other end of the line there came the sound of her sister's voice calling her name over and again, but the only response she could muster was to sob. Magnolia became frantic and shouted down the phone, "What is it? Has something happened to Dahlia?" Azalea finally answered her. "Achak Magnolia, there's no hope for Achak Drölkar. Please come to Lhasa tomorrow. I can't cope on my own."

5

AFTER LEARNING OF THE SERIOUSNESS OF DAHLIA'S CONDITION, Magnolia got on a plane from Chamdo to Lhasa the next day. When she arrived, she went straight to Dahlia's bedside. "Dahlia, look at me. It's Magnolia." She called her name again and again, unable to hold back the tears. How could she not cry when she saw how Dahlia's beauty had been completely ravaged by this brutal illness? Her radiance, her fairness, her supple, curvaceous figure— all were gone and she had been reduced to nothing but skin and bones. She showed no sign of having heard her, so Magnolia called out again, "Dahlia, wake up! It's me, Magnolia." Dahlia finally drifted out of her long unconsciousness, opening her eyes a crack and looking at Magnolia. She wondered if this was a dream, or if she was hallucinating again. *Magnolia can't be here—she's in Chamdo, hundreds of miles from Lhasa. I must be seeing things because I miss her so much.* She closed her eyes again, wearily. She was so weak now that even closing her eyes took a great effort. When they saw the terrible state that Dahlia was in, Magnolia and Azalea held one another, and the sound of their weeping roused Dahlia from her stupor again. She knew now that it was real, and she reached out to Magnolia with a skeletal hand and smiled, the tiniest expression of joy appearing on her face. She tried to gather her thoughts and focus on Magnolia, but she was forced to close her eyes again.

"Has she eaten yet today?" Magnolia asked Azalea.

"Whatever she eats she throws up," Azalea replied through her sniffs. "I made her drink a bowl of milk today, but it came back up straight away. There's nothing left in her stomach now but froth."

A little while later, Dahlia came to again. That afternoon she seemed to improve all of a sudden—her mind was alert and she was talking a lot. Magnolia and Azalea were over the moon, and the three sisters sat and talked for some time, sharing their innermost feelings. Dahlia's mind was still on her parents and her brother.

"If I get out of hospital, I'm going to go back home, work on the farm, and live a peaceful life. My brother's graduating next year. I want to get out of this hectic city and this pointless existence." She went on, sounding serene now, "Birth, old age, sickness, and death—it's a law of nature, and you can't fight it. There's no use in treating this illness now, and I don't want to do it anymore. I'd rather die than keep suffering like this." The other two burst into tears, unable to bear it anymore. They wanted to comfort Dahlia somehow, but neither of them said a word.

Later that afternoon they asked Dahlia what she wanted to eat. "I want a bowl of noodles," she said, "And while you're at it, could you also pick me up a pack of *khyung nga* pills for the swelling?"

Azalea rushed off to find a traditional Tibetan medicine shop to get the pills, then she went and got a bowl of steaming hot noodles, which she brought straight back to her. Dahlia ate the entire bowl with relish; her face flushed with a healthy glow and she perked up even more than before.

"This sickness might not let me go," she said, looking at the two of them, "and I feel like my time is almost up. The thing I'm most worried about now is my brother. He's still a year from graduating, and if something happens to me, I want you two to pass on my money to him. Yangdzom, I want you to call him and tell him I've gone off to some remote place to work for a year, somewhere my phone doesn't get reception. Tell my parents the same. To be honest, if I die, there'll be one less bad person in the world. Every time I think of those women who came to the club at night looking for their husbands, carrying their kids on their backs, I feel ashamed. It's our karma that we ended up in this situation, nothing to do with society, or with this world. The way I see it now, as long as we're not starving to death, we don't need to do that miserable work. If we carry that bad name around with us, we'll never be able to hold our heads up in life, and even if we wash our dirty bodies in the Yarlung Tsangpo, they'll never be clean." Her words were full of contradictions, but it was obvious that she harboured deep regrets about her past actions.

Magnolia smiled wanly and tried to lift the mood. "I told my mum everything. She understood, and she said that as long as your heart is clean that's all that matters. She said that we're young and we don't understand life yet, so if we show our repentance to the Buddha, everything will be okay. In all these years of us being apart, my mum has finally managed to gain a parent's affection for her child. The tears she cried for me washed away all that horrible stubbornness in her, and she treats me with love and kindness now. My heart's not made from stone, either—my parents are old now, and I want to do everything I can to look after them, to put their minds at ease and be by their side. When you're all better we'll still be like sisters, helping each other out, and we'll all have new lives."

That night the three sisters stayed up talking till past ten, at which point Dahlia turned to Azalea and said, "I'm feeling much better tonight, so you go back with Magnolia and get a good night's rest. You haven't been sleeping well the past few days." As they were about to leave, she asked Azalea for the Tibetan medicine pills. Azalea had only been thinking of the noodles and had forgotten to give them to her. She took the packet from her pocket and placed it in Dahlia's hands, thinking nothing of it. At that moment it seemed like she really had got a lot better. Her mind was sharp, and she even looked healthier, so the two of them did as Dahlia asked and returned to their little rented room for the night.

6

THAT NIGHT AZALEA WAS SLEEPING MORE PEACEFULLY THAN she ever had before—right up until she bolted awake at seven in the morning. She'd been dreaming that Dahlia had come into the room with a smile on her face, carrying a big cut of lamb, dressed resplendently in Tibetan clothes and wearing a necklace of coral. She woke with a start and jumped out of bed in a hurry, thinking for a moment it might be real, until it slowly dawned on her that it had all been a dream. Feeling suddenly panicked, she woke

Magnolia and they rushed off to the hospital.

Dahlia was lying still in her bed, her eyes closed as though she were in a deep sleep. The other patient was also sleeping soundly, making the room seem especially quiet that day. Magnolia looked at Azalea and whispered, "Looks like she's still sleeping. Her fever mustn't have been too bad last night. But I think she's been crying—I can still see the traces on her cheeks." When she gently touched her hand to Dahlia's forehead, it was stone cold. Magnolia shook her in panic, and they knew then that she had left them for good and had gone on to another place. The sound of the two girls crying woke the other patient from her peaceful sleep and shattered the tranquillity of that quiet morning on the ward. A few of the little black *khyung nga* pills were scattered next to her pillow and her eyes were shut tight. She looked as if she had no attachment at all to this world, and it was clear now what had happened. The poor girl had left this world for good.

Dahlia was gone. In truth, a prostitute had died. That day, as always, the sky in the city was clear and the beating rays of the sun rose over the mountains in the east.

They arranged a simple service for Dahlia, after which Magnolia returned home. Azalea saw her off at the bus station again, the same one as before, with the same huge crowds. Magnolia was worried about her sister, and as the bus departed, she kept looking over her shoulder uneasily. The last time Azalea had left this station there was still someone waiting for her in the hospital. Now she was all alone, and no matter where she went, no one would pay any attention to her, no one would be waiting for her.

Azalea's weary body was shorn of strength, and as she walked, she felt she could barely lift her legs. She lumbered out of the bus station and headed to a nearby teahouse next to the monument marking the completion of the Sichuan-Tibet Highway. She sat on a bench outside and a waitress came over. "Would you like tea or noodles, Achak?" she asked, then stood waiting for a reply. "I'll have some tea," Azalea said, weak and indifferent. 'When your body's idle, so's your belly,' as they say. In a flash, the girl set a thermos in front of her and she drank a glass of the sweet, milky tea. She had nothing to do now, and all she had left in her pocket was some loose change. She sat at the teahouse for a long time. Looking up and down the street, she noticed a couple of Tibetan restaurants next door where the waitresses were all sitting around outside stretching, smoking cigarettes, and cracking jokes with the men passing by. The girls were wearing the low-waisted trousers that were all the rage in the city in those days, but they couldn't really pull them off, and the dark skin of their midriffs was on full display. They wore no bras under their low-cut tops, so their breasts showed through clearly. Their cheeks were powdered so thickly it looked like they'd smeared tsampa on their faces, the whiteness of the powder emphasizing the darkness of their necks even more, and their lipstick was so red it looked like they'd just feasted on cold livers. Their faces looked like multi-coloured maps, or like they'd been made up of different races and skin colours all stuck together.

It's a funny thing, watching other people. In the past she used to doll herself up to get the attention of men, but looking at these girls now, she felt it was all so pointless. A little while later a couple of men passed by the Tibetan restaurants chatting amongst themselves. A girl in one of the restaurants pulled aside the pink curtain and eyed the younger of the two men. "Brother, why don't you come inside," she called seductively. The man cast her an indifferent, scornful glance, then brushed her off with a derisive laugh and went on his way. The girl shouted after him, "*Oh tsi!* Hey, mister, where'd you get off being so mean? You weren't like this when you came in the other day!" The man's face went bright red, his expression conveying the impression that he'd been unjustly defamed. He stopped in his tracks and glanced at the man who was with him, then went straight up to the girl, grabbed her by the scruff of her neck, and shook her violently. "Filthy whore! Take a good look. Would a man like me come here? Take a look in the mirror before you go throwing accusations around."

He was about to leave again when his friend, looking stunned, said, "What's with you today? Why are you getting worked up by what some street walker says?" This made the man even more angry and he span around, stuck his finger in the girl's face, and hissed at her in Chinese: "Bitch." He turned back to his companion, red-faced, saying something or other in his defence, then stormed off without looking back.

This vile man, who acted the decent guy during the day but had no qualms about going to the brothel at night, looked at the girl with such disdain and cursed her as though he'd been horribly wronged. They don't care what the girls might be thinking, and they certainly don't have any sympathy for them. In the eyes of that man, and of all those upright men in wolf's clothing like him, any woman who sells her body is an animal with no heart, no shame, no self-respect, and no sense.

The girl seemed to be long since accustomed to such behaviour and she didn't look at all offended. She watched him walk off indifferently. "That's right," she said, "You're a man in the day and a monster at night. We might have no sense of shame, but the men who come to us at night are even more shameless." The man likely didn't hear this, and there was no one to respond to it. His outline had long since vanished from her view, just like her words vanished on the faint breeze. She spat out a melon seed shell and went back to chatting and laughing with her friends.

Dahlia's image appeared crystal-clear before Yangdzom at that moment. She remembered what Dahlia had said in those brief moments of lucidity at the height of her agony, tears of remorse flowing down her cheeks: "I have nothing left but resentment and regret for my past. This illness is the only thing that life has left me with." Then she thought of what the doctor had said: "Whatever you end up doing with your life, I think it's best if you give up this sort of work." All these words echoed painfully in her head as though they were fighting one other.

Yes, once a woman is labelled a prostitute, she will forever be a prostitute. She played over these thoughts in her mind as she sat staring down the road that ran away from the monument. There weren't many cars around that day. A small cart bearing a portrait of Guru Padmasambhava that contained some bedding and cooking utensils was passing slowly down the street. Someone was pulling it from the front, and behind, a white-haired nun was making full-length prostrations on the ground as she painstakingly made her way towards the Potala Palace.

The scene before her was so simple and beautiful when compared to the bright lights and the clamour of the Rose. The sight of the elderly nun performing her prostrations was captivating, and she felt the hairs on the back her neck bristle as she was overcome by a sudden feeling of faith. A song sounded clearly in her mind: *I come to you with a pure heart, I come to you with a world of troubles—Oh pure heart, oh troubles—So many lives, so many minds; The true spirit is in us, but if you don't believe, it won't appear—not if your devotion isn't pure...* She watched the old, prostrating nun intently. She couldn't help but well up, and she found herself moving towards the nun, following in her path. The old nun was completely focused, paying no attention to the noise around her as she chanted her *manis* and prostrated with nimble movements. Azalea continued to walk behind her, following the nun's steps. The nun finally registered her presence and stopped her prostrations. She gazed at Azalea with two brilliant, sparkling eyes. Azalea gazed back, her eyes brimming with tears. The nun looked at her for a moment more, her expression one of great love and compassion, then she smiled briefly and returned to her prostrations.

The cart and the old nun faded off into the distance. In the end, they couldn't be seen at all.